EVER

EVER

GAIL CARSON LEVINE

THORNDIKE PRESS
A part of Gale, Cengage Learning

GALE
CENGAGE Learning™

Detroit • New York • San Francisco • New Haven, Conn • Waterville, Maine • London

LIBRARY OF CONGRESS CATALOGING-IN-PUBLICATION DATA

Levine, Gail Carson.
    Ever / by Gail Carson Levine. — Large print ed.
    p. cm.
    Summary: Fourteen-year-old Kezi and Olus, Akkan god of the winds, fall in love and together try to change her fate—to be sacrificed to a Hyte god because of a rash promise her father made—through a series of quests that might make her immortal.
    ISBN-13: 978-1-4104-1024-5 (hardcover : alk. paper)
    ISBN-10: 1-4104-1024-2 (hardcover : alk. paper)
    1. Large type books. [1. Fate and fatalism—Fiction. 2. Gods—Fiction. 3. Winds—Fiction. 4. Immortality—Fiction. 5. Large type books.] I. Title.
PZ7.L578345Eve 2008b
[Fic]—dc22   2008022637

To Bev and Allan, friends forever

ACKNOWLEDGMENT

Many thanks to Betsy Levine for guiding me through the mysteries of knotted rug weaving.

Then Jephthah came to
his home at Mizpah;
and there was his daughter
coming out to meet
him with timbrels and with dancing.
JUDGES, 11:34

. . . dust is their food, clay their bread.
They see no light, they dwell in
darkness,
They are clothed like birds, with
feathers.
THE DESCENT OF ISHTAR
TO THE UNDERWORLD,
MESOPOTAMIAN MYTH

1
OLUS

I am huge in my Mati's womb, straining her wide tunic. She is Hannu, Akkan goddess of the earth and of pottery. My pado, Arduk, god of agriculture, sits at Hannu's bedside, awaiting my birth.

It is too tight in Hannu's belly! I thread my strong wind into her womb, and my strong wind thrusts me flying out. Fortunately, Arduk catches me in his big, gentle hands.

Although Hannu lies in bed and Arduk stands holding me, we are also floating above the earth. In the air over volcanic Mount Enshi hovers Enshi Rock. From its center the temple rises: our home, a tower of porous white stone mounted on four stout stone legs. Never has there been such a temple!

When my diaper cloth is tied in place, I kick. When I'm lowered into my sleeping basket, I cry. If a blanket is tucked around me, I bellow. I am the god of the winds, and I hate confinement. Shame on me! I fear it.

Hannu and Arduk name me Olus. I call them by their own names, as is the custom.

Soon I can see and hear and smell across great distances and through objects, just as the other Akkan gods can. I hear the prayers of our worshipers, which are like the rattle of pebbles in a pan, too numerous to sort out.

When I am a month old, I smile from my parents' bed at the faces of the other Akkan gods and goddesses as they pass by above me. Meanwhile my merry wind tickles their ankles.

But when Puru, the god of destiny, tilts his head down at me, my merry wind fades away, and I wail. His face is swathed entirely in orange linen, as is the rest of him. I can see through ordinary linen, but not Puru's.

Perhaps he can peer through his linen, or perhaps he smells me or only knows I'm there. When he speaks, no constant breath pushes his words, so he stops after each one. "Olus . . . will —"

"Hush, Puru," Hannu says, frowning.

"He's too young to hear about his fate," Arduk adds.

Puru says, "Olus . . . will . . . have . . . no

happiness until he gains what he cannot keep."

2
KEZI

I dampen my square of clay from my bowl of water. Mmm. The water is cool on my hot fingers. Thank you, Admat, for the cool water and the soft clay.

Evening is coming. I'm on the mud-brick floor of our reception room in my pado's house in the city of Hyte. The clay is on a plate in my lap. Using one of my pado's styluses, I'm drawing dancing ostriches in the clay. The ostriches will bob and skip across the next rug I weave. I love to make rugs and to dance.

My aunt Fedo sits in the copper-inlay chair, her leather sack on her lap, her cane leaning against a chair arm. She is telling our servant Nia about buying pomegranates in the market. Nia rests her elbows on the high table. Her face is blank. She smiles only when she is praying.

Looking down at my clay, I scratch in an ostrich leg.

Bang!

Before I can see what happened, I am in Aunt Fedo's arms, and she is limping across the room with me. She is shouting, *"Snake!"*

Nia yells, "Admat!"

I try to turn my head to see, but Aunt Fedo is holding me too tight. She rushes through the door frame to our courtyard. I hear more running feet and Pado and Mati shouting too.

Aunt Fedo yells that an adder was about to strike me. She caned it, but she isn't sure if it's dead.

"I'll get an axe." Pado's feet thud the other way.

Mati takes me and holds me in the air away from her. She eyes me up and down, side to side. When she lets me go, I start back toward the reception room, hoping to glimpse the snake.

Mati pulls me back. "Fedo! Thanks to Admat you were here."

"Thanks to Admat, who gave me owl eyes."

Nia echoes, "Thanks to Admat."

Adders are supposed to have lips like people, and their mouths are supposed to close into a grin. Instead of ostriches, my next carpet will be of smiling adders, doing a zigzag dance.

When Pado returns, he gives me my clay and bowl of water and hands Aunt Fedo her sack. He says the snake is dead. I feel close to tears.

"Your house's omens were mixed today, Senat," Aunt Fedo says to Pado. "The snake was bad, but my cane was good. Perhaps Admat took away the strength in my legs so I could save Kezi."

I separate myself from Mati and take Aunt Fedo's hand. "Come see my new rug." I tug her to the courtyard recess, where my child's loom for rugs sits next to Mati's loom for cloth. "I didn't finish." Above the three dancing mongooses, the top border and my name in wedge letters are yet to be knotted in. I knot from side to side, as I was taught. So the letters of my name will grow gradually, all together, not one at a time.

Aunt Fedo leans back on her heels. "Those mongooses can dance! How old are you, Kezi?"

"Seven and a half."

"My niece is a marvel." She gives me a date candy from her sack. "Have you seen the carpet, Senat? One mongoose is leaping."

Pado nods, but I can tell he's not thinking about my rug. We return to him and Mati.

"Thank you for saving Kezi," Pado says.

He pulls me against his legs.

"Thanks to Admat," Mati adds. "The one, the all."

As I've been taught, I say, "As he wishes, so it will be."

Aunt Fedo says, "Senat, you should hire a masma to cast a spell to rid the house of vermin."

A masma is a sorcerer. I'd love to meet a masma, but Pado would never hire one.

"We'll be fine," he says. He strokes my hair straggles away from my forehead. "Fedo, we're in your debt forever."

Aunt Fedo waves the words away, but Mati echoes, "Forever."

Proud of myself for remembering, I quote the holy text. "A debt unpaid . . ."

"Hush, Kezi," Mati says, sounding nervous.

I hear Nia whisper,

"A debt unpaid is an open wound.
Admat will make it fester."

3
OLUS

I am the god of loneliness as well as of the winds. My brother Lumar, the god of sweet water, closest to me in age of all the gods, is 423 years old. I am eleven, and I have no friends.

From my open-air bedroom on the roof of the temple, I study the mortal children of Akka, listen to their conversations, imitate their speech, practice their gestures. I even starve myself to be as skinny as they are.

My mati Hannu calls me a pretend mortal.

My favorite real mortal is a boy named Kudiya who lives in a hut halfway down Mount Enshi. He is kind and brave, and I want him to be my friend. One moonlit night, I decide to visit him. Before this, I've descended from Enshi Rock only for my annual festivals, and then my parents have come with me on their winged steeds. Whenever I've proposed going alone on one of my winds, my pado, Arduk, has looked worried, and Hannu has pounded her fist into her ball of clay.

But now they're asleep. If they discover I'm gone, it will take them a while to spot me and even longer to saddle their flying horses. None of the gods has true flight. I can ride my winds, and Puru, the god of destiny, can disappear and re-appear wherever he likes, or wherever fate takes him. But the others depend on their mounts.

As soon as I plunge below Enshi Rock on my night wind, I feel the chilly mountain air. Goose bumps rise on my arms. I don't know if they are caused by the cold or by my nervousness.

For at least five minutes I stand outside Kudiya's doorway, gathering my resolve. Finally, I push aside the sheepskin that hangs across the doorway. The hut is tiny. Fear of confinement adds to my unease. I bring my comforting breeze in with me, softly, softly, so Kudiya's parents will continue to sleep. My quiet wind cushions my steps. I crouch next to Kudiya's mat and stare. Wake up! He rolls over and flings out an arm.

I hiss, "Psst."

He slumbers on.

I touch his outflung arm. His eyes snap open.

"Greetings, friend," I whisper. I repeat, "Friend. Friend." I beckon him to follow me.

Outside, he says, "Olus!"

How does he know? In our reflecting pool on Enshi Rock, I look like any mortal boy who's tall for his age.

He shouts at the sky, "I'm having a vision!"

Hastily I cover his voice with my sighing wind. "Sh! I'm really here."

He shakes his head. "You're a vision, and you'll bring us luck all year."

"Touch me, Kudiya."

"In my vision I touch your arm." He does so.

We can't be friends if he keeps thinking I'm a vision. I lift my tunic, pull aside my loincloth, and pee on the grass. "Would a vision do this?"

"Yes! A funny vision!" He shifts his loincloth and pees too. "Tomorrow there will be no brown grass, because I never left my mat."

In the morning he'll know the truth. "Let's race."

We tear through Kudiya's tiny hamlet of five huts. I don't use my winds to speed me along, although Kudiya is swifter than I am.

We approach the Izin, a wide and sluggish river.

"You win," I say.

We push through a forest of reeds and squeeze our toes in the river's muddy bottom. The mud is so soft. My grin feels wide enough to touch my ears.

Kudiya tires of squelching. We return through the reeds to lie on the bank and stare up at the stars and at the underside of Enshi Rock, a small irregular black oval in the midnight-blue sky.

"What does this vision mean?" Kudiya asks.

"I'm not a vision."

"Visions don't tell what they mean. My parents will hire a diviner."

"If I tell you why I've come, will that prove I'm not a vision?"

"No. But tell me."

I hesitate. I've come in the hope he'll be my friend, but I've observed that friendships grow gradually. One person doesn't announce he wants a friend. I try to think of another reason for my visit.

He snores. My cradling wind wafts him back to his sleeping mat while I return to the temple roof, where Hannu and Arduk are waiting.

Even before I land, she shouts. "Where

did you go?"

"Your mati was frightened, Turnip," Arduk says. *Turnip* is his nickname for me, because he created turnips for my first birthday. He adds, "You could have been hurt."

Gods can be injured, although we heal quickly.

"Where did you go?" Hannu repeats, louder than before.

"Just to a hut." I tell them my adventure.

"Turnip . . ." Arduk sighs. "This boy will —"

"Friendship with a worshiper is impossible. Look at the boy tomorrow. You'll see."

I'm sure Hannu is wrong. My parents have little interest in mortals. Hannu doesn't mean to, but sometimes she hurts them. She grows angry when her pottery doesn't go well. If she is angry enough, rocks roll down mountains and fissures open in the earth.

The next day I watch and listen from the temple roof. At dawn Kudiya wakes his parents and pulls them outside, chattering about his vision.

He jumps like a puppet when he sees the brown grass. I laugh until I see his terror. His parents are terrified too. I listen to their conversation. It never occurs to me that I'm spying or eavesdropping. We gods have always watched and listened to mortals.

"He *peed* on our land?" Kudiya's pado says.

"You peed *after* he did?" Kudiya's mati says.

Kudiya nods.

"And then he left?" his pado adds.

"No. We raced to the river."

"You let him win?" his mati asks. "Yes?"

Kudiya shrugs.

"You won! You offended him!" his pado says. "He was angry to begin with, and you made him angrier."

They pray for an hour. I want to fly down and reassure them, but now I understand that I'll frighten them even more. They sacrifice a sheep to me from their meager herd of three. I don't want their poor sheep.

Over the next year I give them all the good fortune I can. I send rain clouds when their land is parched, blow away the clouds when sunshine is needed, keep their animals from wandering. The family prospers.

I don't return to Kudiya or visit any other Akkan mortals.

When I am seventeen, I leave Enshi Rock. I hope to end my loneliness by living among mortals. Because I want to come and go unrecognized, I depart Akka too, although I

23

promise my parents that I'll return yearly for my festival.

Hannu is too angry with me to say farewell. Arduk asks me to down a goblet of therka with them before I go.

Therka is the beverage of the Akkan gods. We enjoy other drinks, too, and eat whatever food we like, but therka satisfies us as nothing else. It contains honey, flower juice, and Enshi Rock water, but the most important ingredients are extracts of each god's and goddess's power. On my ninth birthday, I added wind to the therka.

I gulp down my drink, eager to leave. Hannu sips hers to delay me. When she puts down her goblet, I kiss her. She turns her cheek away but squeezes my shoulder.

"We'll miss you, Turnip," Arduk says.

I nod. I'll miss them, but I'm happy to be leaving. I don't anticipate how difficult it will be to pretend to be mortal.

First I join a camel caravan as a spice merchant's servant. I am kicked by the merchant's camel, then by the merchant. My mischievous wind wants to take revenge, but I do the job myself. While the merchant sleeps, I steal his cargo and fly off on my steady wind. I deposit his little spice bags, one by one, on the route ahead. He will find them, or someone else will cook a tasty stew.

Next I'm hired as a jeweler's helper. I am indoors all day, which I can hardly bear, even though the jeweler's workshop is spacious. I like the man and enjoy his stories about who will wear this necklace and that bracelet. I fancy we're friends and become too zealous on his behalf. When I use my nimble wind to speed the bead drill, he becomes afraid. Trembling, he dismisses me.

I harvest millet. On the second day a sickle gashes my leg. The wound will heal too quickly. I depart before I can become a source of fear again.

Now I despair. I'm not ready to live among mortals, in their very midst. I gather a cloud around myself and ride my winds over the lands surrounding Akka, seeking I don't know what.

Everywhere people are together — except for the shepherds and the goatherds. I decide to try goat herding. I'll still be lonely, but I'll observe people without being observed myself. When I'm prepared, I'll rejoin humanity.

Near the city of Hyte I discover a small valley of good grazing land, part of the estate of a palace official named Senat. The brook that waters the valley is a miracle in this dry countryside.

Senat is willing to rent the valley to me.

"As your flock grows," he says, "give me one kid in ten and you can stay as long as you like."

It's better than a fair rate. I begin my new life with the purchase of a dozen goats and a donkey, paid for with a silver goblet from Akka. I build a pen for the goats to stay in at night and dig a cellar to protect my goat's milk and goat cheese from the heat of the day.

Senat's generosity interests me, so he becomes the first mortal I observe. I watch him in his city house, and my attention is captured. I can hardly look away. My clever wind does my herding.

Senat and his family are what I've wanted. His daughter, Kezi, dances through the house. My eyes can barely keep pace with her feet. She and her mati, Merem, weave together. Merem makes bawdy jokes. Her daughter blushes. Merem's fabric loom turns out tunics and cloaks and scarves, useful and handsome. Kezi's rugs are more than useful. Her subjects are common things — a thistle, three pebbles, a scorpion — made uncommon by her artistry. My favorite is the thistle rug. The flower's spines turn it into a miniature sun, and the hairs on the leaves are an army of silver arrows. Her name in the top border twists cleverly in and out of a leafy vine.

Kezi's aunt Fedo stops by often to lean on her cane and gossip while her sister and niece work. Even Senat joins them now and then. I want to be in the room too. I long to be in Kezi's presence when she dances across the courtyard and when she fingers her goat's-wool thread, choosing a color.

I even wish I could join the family's morning and evening prayers. The mood is serene in the reception room when Senat recites from the holy text of Admat, the god of Hyte. Senat looks to the side of the altar flame, never directly at it. Merem holds her daughter's hand. Kezi sways as if she is longing to dance the prayer. A few servants fidget. The servant Nia, most devout of all, prostrates herself.

Curious, I read the holy text, which astounds me. Admat is believed to be everywhere at once and to be invisible to the living, visible only in Wadir, the land of the dead.

No Akkan god is invisible, and none of us can be in more than one spot at the same time. I wonder how Admat can be everywhere. Is he in my sandal? Or is he my sandal itself? Why would a god bother to be a sandal? Does he wear shoes or sandals himself, invisible ones?

Admat is supposed to know everything, and yet, according to the sacred text, mortals keep surprising him by disobeying his commands. He's forever getting angry at them or forgiving them.

I consider a trip to Akka to ask Ursag, the god of wisdom, about Admat. I want to know if Ursag has ever met Admat or heard reports of him from anyone who has. Chiefly I want to know if there is an Admat at all.

But I don't leave. My god's vision isn't farsighted enough to see Hyte from Akka, and I don't want to miss even a day of watching.

Nonetheless, when something happens, I'm asleep under a tamarind tree. When I awaken, Merem is ill. I jump up, my body straining southward. If I could cure her, I would fly to her bedside on my fast wind, but I have no power over disease.

4
KEZI

My bones hum with fear. Mati didn't rise from her bed this morning. Pado and I are with her. She's shivering with fever and sweating at the same time. She presses one hand into her belly.

Pado paces, which frightens me almost as much as Mati's fever. He's always the calm one. An hour ago he sent for an asupu — a physician. Asupus are called when there isn't much hope.

Admat, the one, the all, pity my pado and me. Let Mati stay with us a little longer. As you wish, so it will be.

There is no sign from Admat. The altar flame is steady. My prayer pulses through my mind, under my other thoughts.

Mati licks her chapped lips. A pitcher of water and a cup rest on a low bronze table next to the bed. The pitcher isn't heavy, but my arm trembles as I pour. I kneel and hold the cup to Mati's lips.

She is trembling more than I am. Although she puts her hand on mine to guide the cup, water sloshes on the floor. She takes a sip or two, then waves me away.

"I don't want to die, Senat. No, I do. I wish I could die. Even the pain hurts, pain on top of pain." She's shaking so hard, her voice rumbles like a cart on broken bricks.

"Hush, Merem," Pado says. "You make it worse."

Beads of sweat stand out on her forehead.

"If only it weren't so hot in here," I say.

Instantly I feel a whisper of a breeze. Startled, I look at the altar flame, which flutters. Does this mean Admat will help us?

Pado sits on the bed and dries Mati's face with his own sweat cloth.

"When I die . . ." She stops to catch her breath. ". . . take a new wife. You need a woman. You need —"

"Hush!" Pado's voice is both pained and amused.

No one but my mati would be bawdy now. Who has such a mati? Let her live!

Pado stands, paces, sits. "I want no one but you."

"I wish Fedo were here. She'd save me"

— Mati laughs jerkily — "or she'd give me something to die quickly."

I too wish Aunt Fedo were here. Except for an asupu, only Aunt Fedo would brave a sick house. She knows remedies for a hundred ailments, and she never treats illness with a knife.

But Aunt Fedo is inspecting her dead husband's land. We don't expect her back for weeks.

Nia appears in the doorway and announces that the asupu has come.

"Bring him in," Pado says.

Nia nods and backs out of the room, her eyes on the altar flame.

"The asupu will make you well," I say with a certainty I don't feel. "Admat, the one, the all, will make you well."

But I'm not sure of this either. Admat himself decreed that everyone dies. I hope he isn't angry with us — or with me. I sin often, although I usually don't mean to.

The holy text says:

Admat's anger, easy to arouse,
Hard to placate.
Beware the wrath of Admat.

Nia returns with an elderly man whose head curls are clearly a wig. He carries a rolled-up mat and a leather sack. Nia kneels at the altar and waits.

The asupu stands on the threshold. "Who is ill?"

No one but Mati is in bed, feverish and shaking. This asupu is too much of a fool to cure anyone.

She laughs. The bed rattles with the force of her laughter.

"Merem . . ." Pado says warningly. He tells the asupu, "The patient is my wife. The illness began suddenly last night and has grown steadily worse."

"Bring candles," he tells Pado. "Fetch a lamb for Admat and bring it here."

Pado nods to Nia, who hurries out. I watch the asupu put his sack on the rug next to the bed and unroll his straw mat. On the mat he arranges the sack's contents: a blue mask, a branch with leaves still clinging, a square of stained wool, the skeleton of a mouse.

I don't mean to, but I picture a tiny asupu, a year from now, carrying his sack into the hole of a sick mouse. From the sack he produces Mati's skeleton, which he will use to cure the mouse.

I squeeze my eyes shut until the frightful vision changes into velvet colors behind my eyelids. When I open my eyes, the asupu is placing a knife next to the mouse's bones. There is a nick in the blade. A nick! A nick will cause a jagged wound. I want to snatch the knife and run out of the house with it.

Pado says, "Merem is an obedient wife. She has the constitution of an ox. She —"

"— a dying ox," Merem breaks in, her voice hoarse.

The asupu frowns. I would smile if I could. Obedient wives don't interrupt their husbands.

Nia comes back with Pazur, another servant. Nia has the lamb, which bucks in her arms. The lamb's legs are tied together, front and back. Pazur has the candles. He puts them down by the asupu's mat and leaves. Nia lays the lamb across Admat's altar. Admat's flame is steady again, although I still feel the faint breeze.

The asupu waves two fingers back and forth in front of the lamb's blinking eyes.

Poor creature! I think, although I shouldn't. Sacrifices are treasured by Admat.

The lamb's eyes close. The asupu guts it, and it makes not a sound.

So that was the purpose of the knife! I am relieved down to my toes.

The asupu reaches into the sacrifice and lifts out the quivering liver. He frowns over it, poking it here and there with his finger.

Meanwhile, Nia lights the candles and arranges them on the floor around the bed. I hear her whispered prayer, repeated again and again. "As you wish, so it will be."

The asupu finishes with the liver. He sets it on the altar and goes to Mati. With his square of wool he wipes the blood from the knife and from his hands. A bead of blood drips onto the mat. The blood is almost black.

Mati has stopped shaking and is lying as still as the sacrificial lamb was. The asupu rubs a strand of her wet hair between his fingers. When he tells her to, she opens her mouth. He peers inside, holding a candle so close, I'm certain he will burn her lips or his wig will catch fire. He touches Mati's abdomen, and she cries out in pain.

I chew on the inside of my cheek until I'm in pain too. I look away, at our mural of the cockroach and the scorpion, which are painted the same size. They are climbing next to each other as if they were friends — to bring good luck. Between the mural and the altar, Nia continues to pray. Her eyes are fixed on Mati and the asupu. I wonder if Nia cares whether or not Mati gets well. Nia exists to watch Admat work his will. But she must care. She was Mati's servant before Mati and Pado married.

I turn back to see the asupu straighten. I hold my breath, waiting for his pronouncement.

But no pronouncement comes. He picks up the mouse skeleton and the branch and ties them together with string. Then he hangs the two in the doorway.

He returns to his mat for the knife, which he holds flat against Mati's jaw, just below her ear.

"This is where I must cut," he says.

I squeak in fright.

"Senat!" Mati cries. "Don't let him —"

Pado is at the asupu's side, his arm around the man's shoulders. "No knife, asupu."

I breathe again.

"You requested my services." The asupu lowers the knife and packs up his sack.

"Isn't there something else?" Pado says.

Mati moans.

"Nothing else." He takes down the mouse skeleton.

I gather my courage. "Can't . . ." My voice is too soft. The asupu is leaving. I speak louder. "Can't it stay?" I want to keep something that may help Mati.

"Did the girl address me?" The asupu sounds astonished.

"Leave the skeleton," Pado says. "Kezi,

35

pay him double. Four barleys."

The asupu rehangs the skeleton and follows me to the dried-foods storage room. I pull aside the curtain. We both have to duck to enter. In the small room I smell him. His scent is gamey, because of his animal sacrifices or because of the human blood he spills.

I give him four pound-weights of barley, each tied in coarse cloth. He accepts them and leaves.

In the bedroom, Nia is still praying. Pado sits on the bed. Mati's face is less flushed than before, but I don't know if this is good or bad. I go to the window. A wisp of cool air whisks across my cheek.

"Now who will cure me? I'll die, Senat."

Pado lowers his head onto her chest. She lifts a hand, perhaps to smooth his hair, but her hand vibrates in the air instead. He reaches up and brings her hand down to the nape of his neck.

Mati smiles at me, a stiff smile. "Kezi, set an example when you're dying. Better than I can."

"I will, Mati. Don't die."

Pado goes to the altar and stops a foot from the cedar platform. He gazes to the side of Admat's flame, as he must.

Nia goes on praying, her words a singsong

36

mumble.

Pado's voice is broken and pitched higher than I've ever heard it. "Admat, the one, the all, god of the children of Hyte, god of everywhere, god of everything, heal my wife. Bless me with your mercy."

Pado, pray longer, I think. Beg Admat. Implore him. Praise him.

Mati cries, "Admat, kill me now."

Nia gasps. I do too. I half expect Admat's flame to set the house afire.

"Admat, kill me now."

I'm surprised at the power in Mati's voice. Some health must remain in her. Admat, forgive her words!

Pado sinks to his knees. "Admat, the one, the all, this worm follows your ways. Pity this worm and heal my wife. As you wish, so it will be."

Mati and Nia and I echo, "As you wish, so it will be."

Pado rises. He turns to the bed, then back to the altar. "Admat," he intones, "god of oaths, hear my vow." His voice grows deep and resonant, his ordinary voice. "Save my wife, and I will sacrifice to you whoever first congratulates me on her recovery."

The room brightens. The walls glow red.

Nia's prayer rises, "As you wish, so it will be."

I feel the room spin and don't know whether Admat is spinning it or my own worn nerves. I grip the windowsill to keep from falling. How could Pado have sworn such a terrible oath?

His voice sounds glad. "Thank you, Admat, merciful one." He strides to Mati and smiles down at her.

Mati raises her head. "You may leave, Nia."

Nia glides from the room.

"It's a dangerous bargain, Senat," Mati says.

"For three days," he answers. "I'll take care. You'll live, and no one else will die."

The oath laws! Pado is using Admat's oath laws. An oath to him is void after three days. If Mati lives and Pado receives no congratulations for three days, no one need be sacrificed.

The holy text says:

Swear on Admat and be blessed.
Admat, protector of oaths.

I'm reassured, until I remember another line of text:

Make not an instrument of Admat.
Use him at your peril.

38

5

OLUS

I sink onto the dry grass. I didn't know they practice human sacrifice here. In Akka it is not tolerated. Hannu sent earthquakes until people stopped.

Apparently Admat doesn't object or hasn't objected in a way his followers understand. Or there is no Admat.

When Senat swore his awful oath, I didn't make the altar flame flare, but I don't control my winds all the time. When they're not needed, I let them go where they will. The flare might have been the result of wind or Admat or an impurity in the lamp oil.

I am overcome by a craving for Enshi Rock, where my fellow gods may be thoughtless but never malevolent. My collecting wind gathers the goats. I untie my donkey from its tether behind the hut and mount it.

"You haven't tasted the grass on Enshi

Rock," I tell the goats as they rise, bleating pitifully, on my north wind. The donkey hee-haws and bucks in fright, and I have trouble keeping my seat. "You'll be glad I took you," I tell the animals. My strong wind blows a cloud our way. We are enveloped in fog, which calms them as they grow accustomed to flight. The goats cease their bleating. The donkey stops braying.

When we are too high to be seen by mortal eyes, I dismiss the cloud and arrange the goats in single file behind me. My tunic billows in the wind. I am the kite and the goats are my tail.

Ha! Admat probably doesn't travel trailed by goats.

I sweep over Enshi Rock. After six months' absence I see it with fresh eyes. The white temple is stark against the cloudless sky. On the roof my canopy ceiling remains in place.

The temple is ringed by terraced gardens, farms, a lake, and workshops for the gods' purposes. A peninsula of land, like an open palm, supports the amphitheater.

What strikes me most, after my time in Hyte, is the absence of mud bricks. Here in Akka, where we have mountains and forests, we build with stone and wood.

I bring the goats and my donkey down in an empty paddock near the stables. Then I muster my courage and start for Puru's hut, which lies between the temple and the workshop of the goddess of love and beauty. I want to see my parents, but first I have questions for the god of destiny.

I've never visited him before. The hut, a single room lit by an oil lamp, is small and windowless. My heart hammers. I must leave!

"Welcome . . . Olus. . . . Sit . . . and stay with me awhile." A chuckle emanates from his orange wrappings. He is seated on a painted chest, holding a tumbler of therka.

With my fresh wind whirling I feel less shut in. I lower myself onto a stool.

Puru lifts a flap of linen to drink, exposing a fringe of mustache. I imagined him clean-shaven, as Arduk and I are.

"Greetings, Puru. I've come from the city of Hyte with questions." I tell him about Senat and his family. "Will my landlord's wife recover? Will anyone be sacrificed?"

He's silent.

"Please tell me."

He shakes his head and his linens rustle. "I . . . will . . . not . . . reveal your fate or the fates of these foreign mortals."

"I didn't ask about my fate." I wait.

He adds nothing.

I'd like to shake him. His hut has made

41

my head ache, but I try one more question. "Where does the god Admat live?"

"I . . . have . . . not . . . heard of such a god."

Outside Puru's hut I breathe deeply and wonder how Merem is faring.

Hannu and Arduk are in Hannu's workshop. When I come in, they embrace me. Hannu's hug is so fierce, I feel trapped. Finally she lets me go and returns to her pottery wheel.

Arduk sits by the long window. He picks up his knife and the block of cedar he was whittling. The shape of a pear is emerging from the wood. "Are you home to stay, Turnip?"

I shake my head, embarrassed.

"He is still the pretend mortal," Hannu says.

"Have you ever met a god named Admat?"

"You're the traveler, Turnip."

As far as I know, no other Akkan god has sojourned in a foreign land or lived among mortals.

I tell them about Admat.

"There are terrible, vengeful gods in the world," Arduk says. "We're not like them."

I explain Senat's oath. "Can we prevent a

sacrifice?"

"Of a foreign mortal?" Hannu says.

I'm too angry to mince words. "You don't care what happens to mortals, not even our own. Arduk doesn't either."

"Turnip" — he puts aside his whittling — "we attend their festivals for us. We —"

"Once a year we let them see us and we answer a few prayers."

"I give them pottery designs." Hannu holds up a double-lipped ewer. "Look at this one."

"But you don't make any new animals for them, and you're not interested in them."

"Not in this one or that one, Turnip." Hannu balls up the clay on her wheel. "Who can be interested in soap bubbles?"

"Mortals aren't soap bubbles. The people of Hyte aren't. Senat loves his wife. Kezi —"

"They don't last," Arduk says.

"You become acquainted with one and *pop!* it's dead." Hannu spins her wheel again. "Pottery lasts."

But it can't feel.

"We should have had children after you," Hannu says, as she has many times. "You would have had godlings to play with."

I agree, although I've never told her so. I'm regretting coming here. Kezi's frightened face, Merem's palsy, Senat's desperation are always in my mind.

On my way to retrieve my donkey and my goats, I pass Arduk's orchid garden. Ursag, god of wisdom and civilization, tallest of us all, is there, peering down at a scarlet orchid. When I was younger, he was my tutor.

I ask him about Admat.

"There's no mention in my tablets of such a god."

"Could he be the greatest god? Could he set the fate of men and other gods?"

"If this Admat were over us, I would know. And fate was written before any gods were born. Puru alone can read ahead." He touches an orchid petal. "Isn't it a marvel?"

"Very nice." I burst out, "A mortal lasts much longer than a flower. Why do we cultivate one and neglect the other?"

He smiles inscrutably. "Your mati raised Mount Enshi from the sea. Your pado planted the first grass seed."

"I don't understand."

"You're so young, you might as well be a mortal. Time passes for you as it does for them."

That's true, but it doesn't answer my question. Or perhaps it does. He is agreeing with Hannu. He also thinks mortals are soap bubbles, not worth helping.

Ten minutes later I am on my donkey, surrounded by my goats, all of us descending toward earth on my sinking wind.

6
KEZI

After Pado's oath, Mati continues to complain of pain, but she stops begging to die. In the evening she drinks duck broth seasoned with thyme.

"Fedo would be happy," she says, giving me the empty bowl and making a face.

Thyme is one of Aunt Fedo's favorite remedies. Mati hates the taste.

I spend the night doing a restless bed dance. I listen for Mati's groans and Pado's footsteps. But the house is quiet.

When I bring her breakfast, Mati says the pain is gone. She sits up in bed. "Thanks to Admat, your pado may not need a new wife."

This is not very funny, but I can't help smiling. She eats all her breakfast and sends me back to the kitchen for a plate of figs. I cover the distance in leaps. My toes hardly touch the floor.

Pado is having his breakfast in the eating room outside the kitchen. He is smiling, too, looking very satisfied with himself.

Nia serves him bread and cheese. Her expression is serious, as always.

"Mati seems better," I tell her, unable to keep silent about the good news. Then I think of Pado's oath. But Nia is safe, because she heard him swear it. Besides, a servant would never speak to Pado unless he spoke first.

Predictably, Nia says, "Thanks to Admat, sower of life, harvester of life."

Pado answers with me, "As he wishes, so it will be."

In the afternoon Mati goes to her loom in the roofed outer square of the courtyard. I'm thrilled, but now the three days of the oath begin.

If someone should congratulate Pado, whoever it is will have to die. The sacrifice is Admat's due. If it isn't carried out, his wrath will fall on Pado and Mati and me and even on my children and their children, down through the generations. Breaking an oath is a grave sin.

Pado could tell people about the oath and then there would be no congratulations. But telling would make the oath empty and would certainly call down Admat's fury.

Doing Pado's bidding, I instruct Nia to sit outside the house and inform anyone who comes that the family is not receiving guests. Even palace messengers are to be turned away. Nia is the right person for this job, I think. Her glum face is not welcoming.

But maybe she'll close her eyes in prayer and a visitor will slip by her.

"Nia, you must be watchful," I say.

"I will not fail in my duty."

Together we carry a chair from the reception room and set it down in the street next to the door. I pick up the yellow sickness mat and take it inside, closing the door behind me. The mat warns people away, but leaving it down when everyone is healthy might cause Mati to suffer a relapse or make someone else sick.

I roll up the mat and place it under Admat's reception-room altar. All will be well. Admat loves his worshipers and we love him. His flame burns as bright in our hearts as on his altars.

The three days will melt quickly into the safe past. I rise on my toes, come down on my heels, spin on my left foot, spin on my right, raise my arms and smile, smile, smile, rejoicing in Mati's recovery.

I'm keeping guard too. From the reception room I can hold off anyone who comes if Nia falls asleep or leaves her post.

If Aunt Fedo had been there when Pado swore the oath, she would protect us. But she's still gone from Hyte and doesn't even know that Mati was ill.

"Kezi!"

I follow my mati's voice to the courtyard alcove. "Does your stomach hurt again?" I ask.

She is weaving. "I feel well. Keep me company."

I sit at my rug loom. "Where is Pado?"

"Where would he be? In his counting room." Mati's rhythm with her shuttle is as swift and sure as ever.

The rug I've been working on is a marriage rug. I meant it as a gift for Belet, my mati's brother's daughter, whose wedding is this afternoon. In the rug a lion stands over a lioness, guarding her. Clusters of dates are strewn at the lioness's side. The dates stand for children and wealth. The rug's border is a river that has no end, for long life. All that remains to be knotted in is the top edge of the river. I've already knotted in my name.

Now there is no hurry, since we aren't going to the wedding. Weaving will keep me here in the courtyard, but I want to have a reason to visit Nia.

Next to my loom is my basket of yarn, a chipped plate, a reed stylus, and a mound of clay in a bowl of water covered by a damp cloth. The clay is there in case I want to plan a change in my rug or design a new one.

With the plate on my lap, I scoop out a handful of clay and flatten it.

"My next rug will be of Admat's altar in the reception room," I tell Mati. I pick up the stylus and begin to draw. After a few minutes I stand. "I have to see the altar." Mati knows that sometimes I must look at my subject so I can portray it accurately.

She nods.

When I get there, I open the street door. Nia is awake, watching Hyte pass by.

"I thought I heard . . ." I say. "I thought . . ."

"No one has come."

Once I am back at my loom, my eyes linger on the wool in my basket. Some shades blend into their neighbors. Others glow against them. I love bright blue next to violet — morning dancing with twilight.

I take up my clay. Half an hour passes.

"Mati . . . I have to look into the reception room again."

"Go."

Nia is annoyed with me. "I know my business, little Mistress. You needn't supervise me."

I retreat. I draw for a quarter hour, then push back my chair. This time I'll see that Pado is safe.

But Mati sees through me too. "Stay. As Admat wishes, so it will be."

"As he wishes, so it will be." I set aside my clay and work on the marriage rug, hoping that weaving will cast its usual spell over me.

Soon the peace of a craftswoman enters me, and I feel the pleasure of Mati's company. I become absorbed in designing my pattern and moving my fingers. Mati doesn't knot, because she makes cloth. I knot, because I make rugs, but we are both weaving. Knotting is weaving too.

Knot. Cut with my weaver's knife. Knot. Cut. Knot. Cut. Count as I go. Change colors. Finish my row. Pass my weft through and pack it down. Begin again.

Mati stretches. "Kezi . . ." She lifts a layer off a pile of cloth at her side to reveal a blue woolen tunic, appliquéd along the bottom with bands of purple wool. The fringes on the purple sash are eight inches long, strung with amber beads. I'm surprised I didn't see her sewing it.

51

"Do you like it?" She holds it up.

"It's beautiful." I've never seen such a pretty tunic. Mati will look wonderful in it. I'd love to try it on. I'm taller than she is, but it would fit me too.

"It's for the wedding," Mati says.

"We can't go!"

"Your pado and I will stay at home, but you may go. A servant will accompany you. Here. Put it on."

"It's for me?"

"For you."

I take it and hold it on my knees. "Oh!" Mati must have beaten the cloth a thousand times to make it this soft.

She pats my lap through the tunic. "I'm thankful to be alive today."

I lean across my new tunic and hug her.

"Go. Try it on and show me how you look."

I drape the tunic carefully over my arm. Mati hangs the sash around my shoulders. I start for my bedroom. When I pass the kitchen, I hear servants chatting as they prepare dinner.

My thoughts turn to the wedding. Until yesterday I'd thought of little else. Belet is marrying my uncle Damki, Pado's youngest brother, a widower fourteen years her senior. Everyone agrees it is an excellent match. Belet's pado doles out spices to all the families in Hyte. Uncle Damki is handsome. He owns as much land as Pado, and he is almost as kindhearted.

Still, if Belet survives bearing children, she will surely outlive Uncle Damki by many lonely years. Aunt Fedo had a much older husband, who died before I was born, and she is alone except for us. She doesn't let us see her sadness, but I know she's sad sometimes.

I want a husband near my own age. My thoughts go to Elon. I've seen him many times in the palace processionals and outside the temple. He's tall and I'm tall. His hair curls naturally, and he's unlikely ever to need a wig.

Of course, I don't know him well. I don't know any young men well, but I have asked a few questions of my friends. One knows someone who knows someone who is his relative, and I have collected a little information.

Elon's parents died when he was a boy. His uncle's house, where Elon lives, is twelve streets away from ours. I've walked there to look. The house also has a red wooden door set into the street wall. A reception room probably lies behind the door, and beyond it a shaded interior courtyard and branching rooms, rugs scattered here and there.

The uncle, who has no sons of his own, has a palace position, like Pado. He buys wooden furniture from the traders who come to Hyte, because few trees surround our city.

Somehow Aunt Fedo knows about Elon. "My owl eyes," she said once, "have seen you wriggle at him."

"I don't!" I was furious. "Aunt Fedo, I never wriggled!"

Pado has said nothing yet, but no girl with wealthy parents reaches sixteen unmarried. Before the end of this year I'll be a wife.

As Admat wishes, so it will be, I think. I enter my bedroom.

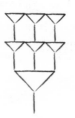

7
OLUS

In her bedroom Kezi spreads the new finery on her bed and smooths it flat. Smiling, she pulls one cloth shoulder higher on the bed, then drags it lower. She does the same with the other tunic shoulder. I'm puzzled.

Her hands skip to the hem. She lifts the hem on one side and tugs that side over the other. The empty tunic is dancing! She releases that side of the hem and lifts the other.

She is charming. I smile with her as the tunic's hips switch from side to side. When the dance is over, she lies on the bed next to the tunic and gazes up at her ceiling, her smile fading, but her hand caressing the fabric.

I wish I could see thoughts.

After five minutes she jumps up and

reaches down to remove her everyday tunic. I never look through clothing, and I will not watch her undress, but I'm eager to see her in the tunic. I withdraw my eyes.

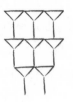

8

KEZI

At two inches above my ankles, the new tunic is the right length. The neck is scooped. The wool molds itself to me. The tunic is modest, but just barely. It is a dress a bawdy mati would make.

I wind the sash twice around my waist and tie a bow to the side, as is the fashion. Slide to the left, bend my left knee. Slide to the right, bend my right knee. I wonder how the tunic looks when I dance. I wonder if Elon will be at the wedding and will see me dance.

Admat, I pray, gazing to the side of the bedroom altar flame, give me a husband I can love. Give me a husband who will love a dancing wife.

The flame wavers, which could be a good sign, a bad sign, or no sign at all.

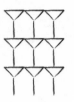

9

OLUS

Nia hasn't left her post. No one has attempted to enter.

Merem is in the counting room, telling Senat that Kezi is putting on the new tunic. He sets down his stylus and follows her to the courtyard. Merem sits at her own loom, and Senat sits at Kezi's.

She must be clothed by now. I glance into her room, prepared to look away, but there's no need. She is holding her round copper mirror and tilting it this way and that to view angles of herself in the tunic.

She is lovely. Her skin is bronzed, a little oily, so she seems to shine. Her eyebrows, her lashes, and her hair are as dark as the Akkan walnut tree, but her eyes are the golden brown of autumn oak leaves. Her nose bulges a little at the end — an olive nose, Hannu would call it.

Kezi's jaw is narrow, but her cheeks are rounded. I think of kissing her cheek and then her lips.

The impulse surprises me. My brother Lumar chases after mortal women, but I don't.

She returns to the courtyard, where her parents beam as she enters.

"Thank you for the finest tunic in Hyte."

"I should have used a different dye for the sash."

"The purple is perfect." Kezi turns for them, a slow dance step. "Is the fit right?"

Merem cries, "You're so pretty!"

Kezi blushes.

"Kezi," Senat says, "your mati tells me you're fond of that boy Elon."

Even Kezi's bare arms flood with pink.

"When this is over" — Senat waves his arm; *this* is the three-day oath — "I'll take the boy out to the fields, see what he knows about crops and channeling the river, see if he's worthy of a beloved daughter. Then . . ." He holds out his arms.

Kezi slips into the embrace.

Senat says into her hair, ". . . we'll see what his uncle offers."

"Ah." My voice startles me, brings me back to myself with the goats. She is on the cusp of transformation, from daughter to

59

wife, a milestone on the mortal road.

They are soap bubbles. Why do I care what happens next? But my eyes return to her.

10
KEZI

I feel my happiness in my feet. My left foot wants to keep me here in Pado's arms, a girl forever. My right foot wants to dance me away to Belet's wedding and then on to my own.

Mati hugs me too. She and Pado are speaking over each other. Mati is saying, "You were such a sweet baby." Pado is saying, "Admat is good to us."

Footsteps and the thump of a cane ring across the reception room. I hear Nia's protests. "No, Mistress. Please, Mistress."

"If there is trouble, I will share it. They can't mean to keep *me* out."

Pado's arms stiffen. Mati's nails dig into my shoulder as Aunt Fedo enters the courtyard with Nia tugging at her shawl.

Aunt Fedo pulls the shawl away. "Stop that!"

Nia goes to the altar, where she mutters prayers.

Aunt Fedo rushes at us, waving her cane. "My sister is sick, and no one sends for me. My sister recovers, and she doesn't tell me."

Pado backs away, but he can't leave the courtyard to escape his oath. If he does, he will break it, and Admat's wrath will be upon us.

"What is wrong, Sister? Why is Nia —"

"We're fine," Mati says. "We only wanted peace for —"

"Peace from me?" Aunt Fedo is insulted. Then she relaxes. "Oh. You thought I was away. I returned this morning and learned you'd been ill." She turns to Pado. "Brother —"

"Aunt Fedo!" I dance in front of her. "See my new tunic! I'm to wear it to the wedding."

"Stand back. Let me look."

I force my knees to support me and make myself smile.

"Turn around for me, slowly."

It's almost impossible to do anything slowly.

"Oh, Kezi." Aunt Fedo places her hand over her heart. "You've grown up. Yesterday you were this big." She lowers her hand. "Today a dozen men will want to marry you." She faces Mati and Pado. "So, Sister and Brother —"

Mati jumps in. "Do you think I should have used another wool on the sash?"

"Why does everyone keep interrupting me? Except Senat."

I'm thinking she doesn't know about the oath and I do. I'm not thinking that I would rather die myself. I'm thinking she rescued me from the snake's bite.

"Brother, you are to be —"

"Pado! Pado, congratulations on Mati's recovery." Admat! My knees buckle, and I faint.

11
OLUS

I roar, "Save her, Admat." One of my goats *maas*.

I send all my winds in search of Admat. The air quiets.

In the house in Hyte, Merem kneels next to Kezi, who is awakening from her faint. Senat, ashen faced, thanks Aunt Fedo for visiting. He guides her out of the courtyard, despite her protests.

No one seems aware of Nia, who is still praying at the altar.

Merem rocks Kezi in her arms. Kezi's face is in her mati's bosom. As Senat comes back in, Merem says, "Kezi can be a priestess and belong to Admat that way."

I know the sacred text better than that, and I'm sure Merem does too. Only Kezi's death will fulfill the oath.

Senat joins his wife and daughter on the floor, puts his arms around them both, and rocks with them.

"Pado?" Kezi breaks out of their embrace and stands, swaying.

Senat rises too. Merem stays on the floor.

"Pado?"

"Yes?"

"Must I die today?"

"No!" I shout.

"No!" Merem yells, as hoarsely as when she was sick.

"No!" Senat bellows.

I want him to declare she'll never be sacrificed. Senat, save your daughter and break the oath. Suffer the consequences if they come.

Kezi wets her lips. "May I go to the wedding?"

"What wedding?" Senat looks bewildered.

"Belet's," Kezi says.

He nods. "We'll all go."

Kezi approaches Admat's altar and stands near the kneeling Nia.

"Admat," Kezi prays, "ruler of the world, I submit to you and the oath that my pado made." Her voice sweetens into a wheedle. "Admat, allow me a little more of my youth. Give me the rest of the fig season. In one moon, in thirty days, when the last figs have ripened, my pado will bring me to the temple." She swallows — I see her throat constrict and expand. "Then the priests will spill my blood for you. Admat, I beg of you, give me a month."

I call my quick wind from the search for Admat and send it to the courtyard altar. The altar flame flares, subsides, and flares again.

Kezi, Senat, and Merem gasp. Nia whispers, "As you wish, so it will be."

I wish one of them would ask for her life to be entirely spared. I wish I could put the words in their mouths. Then I would make the flame bright enough to light up the entire city.

12
KEZI

Admat was merciful. I wonder if he may grant me more time in a month.

Nia, who is at my elbow, bows to me, her face awed. She backs out of the courtyard.

Pado and Mati and I smile at one another.

"See how happy we are to have a month." Mati wipes her eyes. "A month."

"Hush," Pado says. "We're grateful, Admat."

I swallow my tears. I will not spend my last month weeping. "Don't cry, Mati. Did I get dirt on the tunic?"

Mati shakes her head.

"Mati . . . Pado . . . the wedding. We'll miss the priestess's song." I'm dressed, but they must change their clothes.

"Never mind the song," Mati says. "Come with me." She takes my hand and leads me away.

In the family storeroom I stand close to her while she bends over to open a small basket. She says something. I can't concentrate. I hear *caravan, exchange,* and *horse.* Horses are valuable. I've never seen a caravan. I wonder if I'll see one before — I choke off the thought.

Mati opens the basket. Inside is a necklace, which glitters. My vision blurs.

Mati holds the necklace out to me. "Put it on."

Her hands seem to wag back and forth. I feel as if I'm underwater. Mouth open, I suck in air.

"Put it on."

I grasp Mati's arm to keep from fainting again. She pulls me into her. I feel the necklace against my neck and smell her clove perfume. I don't know how long we cling. My dizziness comes and goes in waves.

Eventually I feel better and draw away. "Give me the necklace."

She puts it into my hands in a jumble. My hands drop an inch because I don't expect the weight. I untangle the jumble. Blue and orange gems alternate with gold beads.

"It was for your wedding day." She cups my chin in her hands. "Put it on. Wear it today. My love, wear it today."

While I fumble with the clasp, she searches through a pile of baskets until she finds the one she wants. This one holds a pair of ear-rings, each one a gold crescent moon hung with gold cones. "These were my mati's. Put them on too."

I do. At the wedding I'll be more bejew-eled than the bride.

Mati digs through more baskets. "Every-one will remember my beautiful daughter."

"Mati?"

She looks up from her search, more jew-elry in her hands.

"Did Admat choose me because Aunt Fedo uses a cane, and I don't have a blem-ish?" Sacrificial animals must be without a blemish or they're not acceptable to Admat.

"Admat's ways —" She's crying too hard to finish. The bracelets in her hands clank against one another.

Admat's ways are unknowable. We can't understand his plan, which is always for the best.

She holds out a copper arm bracelet and two silver ones plus a gold ankle bracelet. "Wear everything. People will speak of you forever."

I nod and put on the bracelets. Mati ties my hair with a ribbon of hammered copper.

Before we leave for the wedding, I run to my room and roll up one of my favorite rugs as a wedding gift, since the rug I was working on isn't ready. In this rug, two full-grown date palms stand side by side, their fronds mingling. Next to them are two baby date palms, one a little taller than the other. They are a family, and the mati and pado wouldn't grow so close and share the rainfall if their love weren't strong.

I'm proud of this rug because of my workmanship on the overlapping fronds. Admat! That was hard to do.

Pado and Mati are waiting for me in the reception room. They have put on street faces. Neither one is crying, but their expressions are grim.

"Come," I say. "I'm alive today. Please don't grieve yet."

13
OLUS

My winds return to me. They have been everywhere and failed to find Admat. Perhaps he is insubstantial as well as invisible, and my winds swept through him. Or perhaps he is in Wadir, the land of the dead, where my winds cannot go.

If I can't rescue Kezi by appealing to Admat — appealing to him directly, god to god — I must find another way to save her, with or without him.

Kezi and her parents leave for the wedding. I decide to go too. If an opportunity arises, I will be on hand. The goats will be safe with my minding wind.

I strip off my tunic. Dressed only in a loincloth, I will be a slave at the wedding. Slaves are all but invisible, almost as unseen as Admat. No one expects a slave to be an acquaintance. Senat won't recognize me if I don't draw attention to myself. Everyone will think I belong to someone else.

My south wind takes me high above Hyte, high enough for anyone who looks up to think me a bird. When I reach my destination, I wrap myself in fog. My downwind deposits me in a deserted alley. The alley is too narrow for comfort, but I endure it. I watch my feet and ignore the encroaching walls. The alley winds to the King's Road, the broad avenue that leads from the city gates to the palace. The wedding is in the open air, in the avenue.

I've observed many Akkan weddings, but I've never watched one in Hyte. I hurry along the seven-foot-high wall that lines the King's Road. Luckily, the wedding guests have their backs to me. They face a priestess who is singing praises to Admat. Nearby is a recess in the wall, which I slip into. From its shadow I watch for something a slave can do. Kezi and her parents haven't yet arrived.

The priestess's voice is high and piercing.

"Thanks to Admat,
Maker of Damki,
Maker of Belet . . ."

Several children play and squabble on the outskirts of the guests. Their piping voices mingle with the priestess's song.

Long tables, placed end to end, extend down the middle of the street. A skinny yellow dog sits near a table, nose up, waiting. A parade of a dozen male servants and slaves turns out of an alley across from me. The servants wear coarse tunics and sandals. The slaves wear loincloths and are barefoot.

I slide out of my sandals.

Slaves and servants alike carry trays of covered bowls and plates, which they arrange on the tables. They return to the alley. Since the tables aren't filled, I assume they have gone back for more. When they return, perhaps they'll stay, and I'll find some unobtrusive occupation.

Kezi and Senat and Merem enter the avenue from their street. Kezi gives the rug she is carrying to Merem and hurries toward the celebration. Her blue tunic glows in the sunlight. I don't know what the effort is costing her, but she is smiling.

She passes by without seeing me. Her cinnamon scent is in the air. I could run out and touch her. We are together. Not truly together. Apart, but I am with her.

14
KEZI

The priestess finishes her song as I reach the cluster surrounding her.

". . . Of all happiness.
Thanks to Admat."

Her listeners turn away. I see the bride and groom, Belet and Uncle Damki. Belet looks lovely in a purple tunic. Uncle Damki is almost as handsome as Pado. I smile and wave.

Belet sees me and waves back.

My eyes fill in spite of myself. I pretend a stone has gotten into my slipper. I bend over and adjust the felt. When I straighten, Aunt Fedo is hugging Belet. Now I'm furious. If Aunt Fedo weren't so strong willed, Nia would have been able to keep her out.

A musician shakes a copper rattle. I seem to hear each bead strike metal.

Admat, I pray, let me savor my cousin's wedding. Let me savor everything until I have to die.

The rhythm of the rattle enters me. I bend my knees and bob gently. A circle forms around Belet and Uncle Damki. Mati and Pado stand on either side of me. Aunt Fedo is directly across from us. She smiles and waves. I smile back. She is still my beloved aunt.

To the left of Aunt Fedo, separated from her by two men, is Elon, whom I might have married. Why did I like him so much? He has a curly beard, and I prefer a clean-shaven man. His posture is poor. Aunt Fedo says a man who doesn't stand straight is selfish.

A smoke diviner joins Belet and Uncle Damki and lights incense in a censer. This is the most anxious moment in the wedding. Smoke streams out of the censer. The diviner will observe the smoke designs and announce whether or not the marriage omens are good. If they are bad, the wedding will be called off, even now.

A breeze blows across my neck. The smoke writhes and throbs with the rhythm of the rattle. It forms waves, spirals. It widens, then narrows. I've seen smoke come from a censer before, but never like this.

This smoke seems alive. The diviner's eyes are enormous. She's never seen anything like this either. People whisper around the circle.

The diviner clears her throat, looks down at her hands, up at the sky. Her reputation will suffer if she can't interpret the omens. "The portents are excellent," she says at last. "The groom and bride will love each other forever. The bride will bear a dozen healthy children."

Everyone sighs with relief, except Mati and Pado and me. We're part of the wedding and not part, here and not here.

A priest enters the circle, bearing a clay tablet. On the tablet rest two ripe dates and two balls of barley soaked in vinegar. The dates represent the joy in marriage. The sour barley balls represent the difficulties. The marriage contract has been written on the tablet in tiny wedge letters.

I've seen my parents' marriage contract many times, although I can't read it. I can write only my own name and can read only the names of my parents and Aunt Fedo and Admat.

The priest intones three times over:

"The omens are favorable,
But the outcome is with Admat.

As he wishes, so it will be."

Belet pops a ball of barley into her mouth. "I will endure any trouble that comes."

I taste the vinegar in Belet's mouth. I'll never be a wife.

Uncle Damki holds a date up to Belet's lips. She opens her mouth and takes it in. I taste the date too.

"I will be a sweet wife. I am your wife."

Next, Uncle Damki eats the barley and the date. "I will endure the bitterness. I will welcome the sweet. I am your husband."

They are married. I cheer with everyone else.

Belet begins to dance. Uncle Damki backs away from her. The women circle her and dance too. At last! Mati and I join in. Pipes and a lyre accompany the rattle. A singer begins to wail.

Several men stand outside the circle and watch. A few step from side to side, snapping their fingers.

Right foot behind my left. I dip, my eyes half closed, losing myself in pleasure. Left knee raised, higher than the other dancers', higher than the bride's, I point my toes in my felt slipper. Bend at the waist. Three steps back. Straighten. Raise my arms. Toss my hair. Make my bracelets and earrings jingle.

The song ends, but the singer starts another one, and the musicians join in. Mati can't catch her breath. She squeezes my hand and drops out of the dance. I continue.

Elon is among the men who are watching the women. His eyes follow me. I blush. A slave is sweeping and watching me too.

My blush deepens. The slave is flawless, without a blemish. Majestic, taller than Elon, more muscular. I am only peeking at him and looking away and peeking again. But since the slave wears no tunic, I see that his muscles are powerful but not blocky. He stands straight, and he is clean-shaven so I see his square jaw and his wide mouth.

Aunt Fedo says a wide mouth means deep feelings. I think Admat gave me Aunt Fedo's owl eyes today, because I see humor and sadness in that mouth.

The slave shouldn't stare at me. While he stares, he sweeps across Elon's foot.

Elon kicks him hard in the shins, and he almost falls. I stumble. The slave regains his footing. So do I. He bows to Elon and says something, which must be an apology. He glances at me to see if I was watching. I lower my eyes.

I am glad I will never marry Elon.

Elon ignores the apology and looks back at me. I turn my head to the right and lift my chin. The rhythm of the rattle becomes faster and more complex. I forget both Elon and the slave.

15
OLUS

She's seen me! Except for the young man who kicked me, no other guest has noticed me, and I'm certain the young man forgot me as soon as he finished applying his foot to my legs.

She saw me! I wonder if she thought about me longer than the young man did. I am thinking ridiculous thoughts, but I hope she liked me. She had no time to form an opinion, and she has much more to think about than me, but I hope she liked me.

If I sweep much longer, someone will find it odd. The slaves and servants have noticed me already. I don't think I'm in danger from them, as they are unlikely to speak to their masters. I slip back into my wall recess and look for something else to do.

Merem is at the edge of the circle of female dancers, watching Kezi. Aunt Fedo joins her for a while and then moves away.

Merem remains. Sometimes she smiles. Sometimes her eyes fill.

Senat watches from the vantage point of the beer vat. I hear him boast to the other drinkers about Kezi's grace and mastery of the dance. He brings the beer straw to his mouth too often and weeps openly. Then he grows silent. He doesn't tell anyone his daughter's fate.

She dances for hours. I imagine carrying her to safety on my strong wind. But I fear that the wrath of Admat would be unleashed against her and her family. If I were sure there was no Admat, I would fear nothing.

I wonder what Hannu and Arduk would think of her.

They'd call her a soap bubble, but what else? A heroic and exquisite soap bubble? A soap bubble worth saving?

It doesn't matter what they think. Somehow I will save her.

16
KEZI

The sun sets. Torches are lit and held by slaves. I whirl, sway, and step, step, step. While I dance, I am free of my fate. Admat moves with me, and he is eternal.

But finally I need food and drink more than I need to dance. I bow at the waist and stop. Mati wraps a shawl around my shoulders. The night air is cool. The shawl is linen, embroidered with purple thread. I run my palm across the smooth cloth, then touch Mati's cheek to thank her for the shawl. I want to feel everything.

Mati leads me to the feast tables and loads a plate for me with goat cheese, onions and lentils, millet bread, and mutton spiced with mustard.

The bread breaks in my hand — proof of its freshness. I devour it and spear a chunk of mutton with my knife. The mustard is sharp, the mutton moist and gamey, baked to the melting point. I've never tasted anything so good.

The musicians stop playing. I hear Uncle Damki's shout of laughter. A young pig roots under the table. I see its back legs and its spotted rump.

The magnificent slave stands at the other side of the table a yard away, stacking dirty dishes. Out of the corner of my eye I watch him as I eat.

He collects two tall piles of plates. He'll take the plates and go, although I want him to stay. Like the joy of dancing and the delicious food, his magnificence holds off my grief. I wonder if he belongs to Uncle Damki or to Belet's parents.

He doesn't go — as if he heard me want him not to! Instead he begins to unpile the dishes, re-creating the mess he has just cleaned up.

I'm so surprised, I nudge Mati.

"What is it, love?"

He stops moving.

"Never mind." I don't want to cause him trouble. I take my last bite of mutton. My plate is empty.

Mati takes it away and entwines her arm in mine. "I think we should congratulate Belet's parents."

Her parents have sworn no oath that they

mustn't be congratulated. I don't want to see their joy. I don't want to speak about Belet and Uncle Damki, who have years ahead of them. I free my arm from Mati's. "You go."

"I don't want to leave you."

"I'll be fine."

She goes. The slave is piling dishes again. Why?

Several other wedding guests — no one I know — are taking food, but they don't seem to notice him. What if he is invisible to everyone but me? What if he is my guardian, sent by Admat to watch over me in my last days?

I doubt this, but I risk smiling at him.

He drops a plate.

It plummets. But then, in the instant before it strikes the baked mud street, it hovers in the air and comes down softly, unbroken.

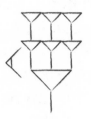

17
OLUS

I am furious with myself. I didn't intend to use my small wind to catch the plate — I did so automatically.

Kezi is staring openly at me. I shrug and smile apologetically. She doesn't smile back.

When she smiled at me before, I felt we were somehow allies. Our alliance is spoiled now, but she doesn't give me away.

"Kezi!"

She turns. I retrieve the fallen plate.

Aunt Fedo is coming toward her with the fellow who kicked me. "This young man has been begging to be introduced to you." I see she is proud of herself for bringing him. "He says you are the most beautiful girl here."

He puts his fist to his forehead to show his respect. "Anywhere," he says. The fellow

85

kicks slaves, but he is gallant.

Kezi bows her head briefly. I think she doesn't like him either or she would smile.

"Kezi, daughter of Senat and Merem, meet Elon, nephew of Ibal and Gazu."

He is the man she might have married!

"Are you enjoying the wedding, Kezi?"

"I'm happy for Belet and Uncle Damki."

Aunt Fedo cocks her head. "My rabbit ears hear my name." She takes two figs from a bowl on the sweets table and gives one to Kezi and one to Elon. "Soon dates and barley," she says, smiling conspiratorially at each of them. Then she leaves.

Gallant again, Elon offers his fig to Kezi. She jumps away as if the fig were a scorpion. "I hate figs." She gives hers to him and wipes her hands against each other.

He eats the figs quickly, seeming to swallow them whole, as a wolf swallows a sand rat.

The singer starts to wail again, and the musicians to play.

"Will you walk with me?" He gestures down the dark avenue, away from the crowd and the torches.

"No, thank you."

"There is nothing wrong in it. Your aunt Fedo said your esteemed pado will speak with me."

Her shoulders go up. I think that if she had wings, she would leap into flight. She says nothing.

"Come, I beg of you. I prayed to Admat that you would come."

She nods.

They walk. It is a black night with no moon, but I can see them. Kezi's step is graceful. She dances even when she walks.

He adds, "Thanks to Admat."

"As he wishes, so it will be."

They fall silent, but there is a little drama in the way they walk. He tries to stay close to her side. She zags away. He zigs near again. They began in the middle of the avenue but swerve toward the wall.

I have piled dishes long enough. I take the broom again. Making silent sweeping motions an inch above the ground, I follow Kezi and Elon. In a moment I am beyond the dim torchlight. My low wind lifts me so my feet are silent too.

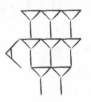

18
KEZI

Elon says, "Your necklace is superb."

I dislike even his whispery voice.

He adds, "It would befit a bride."

I laugh. I'm wearing it because I never will be a bride.

"Did I offend you?" He sounds offended.

I swallow my laughter. "No. It was nothing. I'm sorry."

"I meant *my* bride. Your mati shouldn't have let you wear it on a lesser occasion. It should be kept safe."

I don't answer. He stops walking. I turn, wondering why.

His hands grasp my shoulders. "I would hate to offend you."

I try to shrug him off, but his grip is firm. I pull back and feel the wall behind me.

"If we are almost betrothed, I can kiss you. When I watched you dance . . ." The dark oval of his head comes at me. I can barely make out his parted lips, the faint gleam of his teeth.

I shout for help, but I'm sure we're too far away for me to be heard. I cry, "Admat!"

One of his hands lets go of my shoulder and presses on the back of my head. His teeth clink against mine. His breath smells sour.

Then his mouth is gone. His hands are gone. A wind blows along the avenue. I wrap my shawl around me to keep it from flying away. Two figures are struggling.

Elon groans. I hear a thump. The wind dies. One of the figures is at my side, taller than Elon. In the dark I can't tell if I recognize him. Too late I think of running.

"Mistress . . ." The voice is hardly louder than a whisper, but it's deep and it seems to echo. "Pardon me." He has an accent. His *p* sounds like a *b. Bardon me.* I don't know anyone who speaks with an accent. "Did he hurt you?"

"No. Thank you for rescuing me." Who is he? "Thank you." I am grateful enough to thank him a thousand times.

"Good. Er . . . good."

"Is Elon . . . Will Elon —"

"Elon is only stunned. He'll sleep awhile. I'm glad you are fine."

"Thank you. How did you know? Did you hear me shout?"

"Yes, but . . . er . . . I followed you."

If he hadn't just saved me, I might be frightened that he followed us. No. How can I be afraid of someone who sounds afraid of me?

"Why did you follow us?"

"I didn't trust him. He kicked me."

My savior is the handsome slave! "You're the . . . You pile dishes and unpile them." Maybe Admat did send him.

He laughs. "I'm not a slave."

Why pretend to be one?

"I'm . . ." He hesitates.

My guardian?

"I'm a goatherd."

He can't be!

"I am Olus, son of Arduk and Hannu." Foreign names. "I rent grazing land from your pado."

Now I am a little frightened. "How do you know who my pado is?"

"You arrived together. And I heard your aunt say."

Ah.

He adds how generous Pado has been to him, and then I know he is telling the truth. I tell him my name. We start back to the wedding.

In the distance the musicians are still playing. My slippers *shush-shush* on the baked mud street. His bare feet *pat-pat.* My heart does a *pat-pat* too. Although I can't see him clearly, I am aware of how glorious he is.

I wonder why I didn't hear him following us. Then I remember the plate he dropped, the plate that hung in the air before touching the ground.

I want to ask him about the plate and his silent feet and why he's pretending to be a slave and why he came to the wedding. Most of all I want to ask him if he is my guardian. But I'm afraid to. Instead I say, "Where is your pasture?"

"Close to the northern boundary of your pado's land. There is a brook."

"I know where." Pado let him have a good spot. "Every autumn we spend two weeks nearby. I love to walk into the hills."

"I wish you could see a wedding in Akka, where I come from."

I've never heard of Akka. "Are your weddings different from ours?"

"Some parts are identical. There is a marriage contract and eating the bitter and the sweet. But in Akka we have a pantomime. The bride and groom hold hands. Someone — perhaps a friend of the groom — dons a gray tunic. He is Storm. He attempts to tear the couple apart, but they hold fast. Another friend wearing black is War. She tries to separate them, but they hold fast. Someone else may be Gossip. Two mort— Two people may be Children Arguing."

I love this. "What does Gossip wear?"

"Gossip doesn't have a costume, but Gossip claps together the jawbones of a donkey."

"Is there music?"

"Drums."

"Do the bride and groom always hold fast?"

"They never let go."

I wish Olus had kissed me instead of Elon. The most daring thought comes to me. I can't act on it.

But Admat sends everything: my thoughts, my feelings, my death, this goatherd. So perhaps I should. Tomorrow I will have twenty-nine days left.

"Kezi, I —"

"Olus, will you erase Elon's kiss? Will you kiss me?" I hold my breath, waiting.

His feet stop their *pat-pat.* Have I shocked him?

His hand tilts my chin up, so gently.

I close my eyes and give myself over to his touch. His other hand, gentle too, cups my cheek. He kisses me, a feather kiss. His breath is sweet. He kisses me again, longer.

I lean into his chest.
  A wind picks us up, and we rise.
  I am filled with terror.

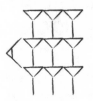

19

Olus

She screams, "Admat!"

My high wind blows her scream into the sky. Again I didn't mean to use my winds. She pushes away from me and starts to fall. I catch her around the waist and bring her down slowly. She runs from me.

She runs until she reaches the nearest of the feast tables, which is deserted. For several minutes, which pass like months, she lingers there. Then she turns my way. To my amazement, she smiles.

I rise on my merry wind and smile back, although she cannot see.

She points her toe, turns her foot to the side, raises her arms, and performs a brief leaping dance. When she's finished, she joins the dancers again.

Did she like our kiss?

20
KEZI

After the wedding I sleep into the afternoon. I awaken thinking of Olus.

Sleep has brought understanding. There is no mention in the holy text of Admat ever sending guardians to people. I am not so extraordinary that he would send one to me.

Olus must be a masma, a sorcerer — a foreign masma because of his accent and his foreign name. This explains everything: how he kept the plate from breaking, how he followed us without our knowing, how he so easily defeated Elon, how he raised me in the air.

Masmas are people, like everyone else. Most are believed to be bad, but some are decent, even devout. Olus couldn't be evil, or Pado would have known. Pado wouldn't rent his land to an evil person.

Olus may be able to fly much higher than he lifted me. What marvelous magic!

I wonder why I caught his interest. Is he

thinking of me right now? Or of his goats? Probably his goats!

I stretch in bed. My legs are sore from so much dancing. I would love to dance while flying. Mmm, mmm. Such a thrill to leap a mile, to touch a cloud.

These may be sinful thoughts, but I don't see why.

I sit up.

It is as if yesterday were in a corner, waiting to pounce, and now it does. I hadn't forgotten the oath and the sacrifice, but I hadn't looked in that corner until now.

I slump back and roll over, pressing my face into the mattress. My tears seep through the sheet into the wool stuffing. Soon I smell wet sheep. I can't stop crying.

Mati comes in and sits next to me. She pulls me against her and rubs my back.

"Will . . . will . . ."

"What?"

"Will . . . will . . . the knife . . . hurt?" The priest's knife.

She holds me at arm's length and touches the tip of my nose the way she used to when I was little. "Admat won't let it hurt."

Maybe he is so angry with me that he wants it to hurt.

Pado parts the curtain that crosses my

doorway. When he sees us crying, he runs in. He kneels at my bedside. The three of us weep, clinging to one another.

After a while he pulls himself up and sits on the bed, too. The bed groans under the weight of all of us.

I have no more tears left, so I laugh. "The bed will collapse."

"No matter," Pado says.

The bed has to last only a few more weeks. Of course, that's not what he meant.

Mati says, "Aunt Fedo came while you slept."

"We told her," Pado says. "She's weeping, too."

"She's here? Where?"

"In the reception room," Mati says.

I don't want to see her.

But I do see her. Mati and Pado wait outside my room while I dress in my everyday tunic, which has a green stain at the hem.

Aunt Fedo is in the copper-inlay chair, head down, looking into her lap. When she hears us, she tries to stand but drops her cane. She bends over to reach for it. Her back shakes with sobs.

Through her tunic I see the bumps of her spine. Her hair is as much gray as brown. How many more years have I given her?

We may both die tomorrow, in spite of Pa-do's oath. As you wish, so it will be.

21
OLUS

Last night, as I rode my north wind back to my goats, I thought of a glimmer of a plan for how Kezi may be saved, but the plan has a thousand obstacles, and I may be one of them. Before we can face the obstacles, I have to speak to her again, and I don't know how to accomplish even that.

I sit at the edge of my brook and watch her. She squats by her aunt's chair and puts one hand on her aunt's knee. "Aunt —"

Aunt Fedo straightens. "My rabbit ears heard Nia tell me to leave. Why didn't I listen?"

Kezi smiles. I think I understand why. I've observed that Aunt Fedo's rabbit ears hear well, but often they don't listen at all.

"You spared my life! Oh, Kezi . . . Kezi . . . thank you."

Kezi's hand on Aunt Fedo's knee turns palm up.

After a long pause Merem says, "Kezi

hasn't breakfasted yet."

They go to the eating room, which faces the alley behind the house. Senat and Merem and Aunt Fedo have their second meal of the day while Kezi has her first. It's simple fare: sheep cheese, barley flatbread, roasted onions, and sweet cucumbers. Kezi closes her eyes while she sucks on the cheese. The others begin to tell stories. While they talk, one or another touches Kezi's shoulder or her cheek or adds more food to her plate.

Their first tales are about her when she was a baby.

"You were motionless only when you slept," Merem says. "You hardly ever cried."

"I used to keep you with me in the counting room sometimes."

"Pado, you did?"

"If you could wave your hands and kick your feet, you were happy. I'd stand over you and watch when I should have been planning crops."

"You never crawled," Aunt Fedo says.

Merem corrects her. "Once or twice you crawled."

Aunt Fedo ignores the correction. "You were too eager to walk and dance."

"And climb!" Merem says. She pats Kezi's hand.

Senat, Merem, and Aunt Fedo laugh.

"Nothing was safe from you," Senat says, breaking off a section of bread for her.

"Once when Aunt Fedo and I took you to the market . . ." Merem begins.

Aunt Fedo says, "I had nothing to do with what hap—"

"Almost happened," Merem says.

"What happened?" Kezi looks from one to the other. She seems happy.

They all seem happy. How can they be happy? But I notice that I'm happy too, listening and watching.

They tell the climbing story, in which Kezi almost poked her face into a hive of wasps. Then Aunt Fedo tells about Merem when Merem was a little girl. Senat and Merem talk about their courtship. Merem can hardly speak for laughing over an occasion when Senat set his beard on fire.

"Because he was looking at me!" Merem says, gasping for breath.

Senat blushes.

Kezi blushes too, and it occurs to me that she is thinking of me. But she couldn't be.

They remain in the eating room all afternoon and into the night. My fresh breeze ripples through to keep them comfortable. They have a wonderful day. We all have a wonderful day. Sometimes Kezi looks away while her aunt and her parents speak. Her face is alert and peaceful. I'm certain she's concentrating on their voices. Sometimes she watches their faces, her eyes passing from one to the other.

Senat never goes to his counting room. Merem and Kezi don't work at their looms. Aunt Fedo doesn't leave to manage her own affairs. It's a holiday, a holiday because Kezi is to die, but a holiday nonetheless.

22
KEZI

The next morning I go to my loom. Mati is already working. On my loom is the marriage rug. I hate the sight of it, but I begin to tie my knots. Even now, I cannot waste so much work.

Mati's yarn tangles. For a few minutes she tries to untangle it. She calls herself bumble-fingered, then calls herself cursed, then looks at me, her face stricken, because I'm the one who's truly cursed. She runs from the courtyard.

I sit back in my chair, my hands in my lap. I don't want to weave or even to move. If I could, I would turn myself into the lizard that's sunning itself on the edge of a fern pot.

Nia comes into the courtyard to water the ferns. The muscles in her thin arms stand out from the weight of the copper watering pitcher.

Once, when I was five, she found me playing with a doll that I had stood on Admat's altar in my bedroom. She rushed at me and pulled me away, scolding that the altar was not a place for games. My doll fell on its head, which Nia said was my punishment. She prayed over me until Mati called her. I've always wondered how long she would have prayed if she hadn't had to stop.

Now I want to know what she thinks of my sacrifice. She is the most pious among us. Maybe she can explain my sacrifice in a way that will comfort me.

"Nia?"

She puts down the pitcher.

"Why has Admat made this happen to me?"

"Ah." She smiles. "Little Mistress, Admat wants you to dance for him alone and make rugs for him alone." She picks up the pitcher again and begins her task.

She's made Admat seem selfish.

Maybe he will prove himself unselfish and extend my life.

I don't hear Pado until he pulls Mati's chair away from her loom and sits in it. He strums the warp of the loom as if it were a lyre.

I want to ask him about Olus: How long has Olus rented our land? Does he take good care of his goats? Does Pado like him?

But Pado will ask how I know there is a goatherd.

He sings softly,

"Admat, the king's king,
The man's master,
The child's pado,
Who . . ."

His voice breaks.

". . . cares for us all."

He weeps, stands, and wanders away from me toward his counting room.

I don't know how I will bear to spend my last month with my parents' unceasing sorrow.

23
OLUS

I watch Kezi through her sad day. Aunt Fedo visits again and takes her turn in Merem's weaving chair. She is silent for the first time in my knowledge of her. After half an hour, she rises and goes to be alone in the reception room. They are each alone today: Kezi motionless at her loom, Senat in his counting room, Merem on her bed, Fedo in the reception room.

I with my goats.

In the evening I send my clever wind to Akka.

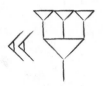

24
KEZI

As I'm falling asleep, I wonder if Olus might be able to help me live beyond the twenty-seven days I have left. Maybe Admat sent him to me for that purpose.

I don't know what magic a masma can do. Perhaps a spell could make someone swear an oath that goes the opposite way from Pado's. Whoever fulfills the new oath will have a long life. With Olus's aid I could fulfill the second oath.

Or Olus could cast a spell to slow time just for me. With such a spell I would live for years in my remaining days. Lonely years, unless he slowed time for himself as well.

These are my foolish thoughts. Still, he is a masma.

And I am half in love with him.

At breakfast I tell Mati that I would like

to visit the market. I must escape our sad house for a few hours.

"I'll come."

"No need."

She nods.

To go into the street without Mati or Pado, I must bring a male servant. I pick Pazur, although I know he wouldn't be Mati's choice. Pazur has many friends. Some will be at the market. He'll chat with them, and I'll be free of him.

Before we leave, while Pazur waits in the reception room, I run to my room. My everyday tunic is good enough for the market, but I change into my second-best — my best until Mati gave me the blue one. Second-best is pale purple with a white belt and white embroidery along the hem. I tie my hair in a ribbon and toss a few copper coins into my small tapestry sack, which I tie onto my belt.

I remove my felt slippers and put on sandals. The market is near the city gates, a long way from our door.

We join the throng on the King's Road. I smell the market before we reach the first stalls: spices, smoky grilled meats, sweat, hides, wool. I see the striped awnings that shade the street from the summer sun.

"Pazur!" A young man waves to him from

shoulder-high stacks of baskets.

"Go," I say. "I'll find you when I'm finished."

Pazur nods and is off.

Someone is shaking timbrels. Someone taps a drum. Stepping high, almost dancing, I follow the sound.

Chickens flap in their cages. The turtle woman stands by her wide bowl of turtles. Half a dozen men stand at the beer vat, paying their coins for pulls at the straw. Children cluster nearby, waiting their turn at the plum-juice vat.

The musicians are playing next to a market cook, who is grilling goat meat on an open brazier. Poor musicians. Several people are eating the cook's wares, but no one is listening to the music. The musicians' coin cup is empty, and no wonder. Their rhythm isn't interesting, although they gesture as the masters do. The drummer leans over her drum and shakes her hair. The timbrel shaker squeezes his eyes shut in concentration. He raises his arms and sways. The fringes of his shawl skim close to the cooking meat.

Out of pity I put a coin in the cup and step side to side along with the simple beat. Something bumps into my toe. A ball of yellow wool! I bend over. Although the ground is level, the ball rolls away, trailing a strand.

My heart *pat-pat*s again. I follow the strand.

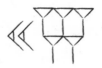

25
OLUS

My ground breeze rolls the ball of wool toward me. Kezi follows. Outfitted as a wool peddler with a deep basket of yarn, I wait outside the city gate.

The wooden gate doors have been pushed inward because the city is open. Facing outward to the right and left of the gate are twin colossi, enormous stone lions with bearded human heads. I stand under the beard of the right-hand lion.

My scheme had been to peddle my wool down Kezi's street, but when I saw her making her way to the market, I came here.

The ball of wool unwinds past the furniture makers, the sellers of remedies, the scribes for hire. Then it veers left, away from the stalls, beyond the water trough for the merchants' donkeys and camels, and down the deserted final stretch of the King's Road. When the yarn rolls through the gate,

Kezi hesitates.

I send the wool back to her and dismiss my ground breeze. If she fears leaving the city, she can take the yarn and go. I'll find another way to speak to her. I don't want to frighten her again.

She picks up the wool and rolls the strand onto the ball. The yarn is speckled with gold. She scratches a speck with her fingernail. I performed the same test myself. The gold won't come off.

"Olus?" She rounds the lion's huge paw.

She knew it was me! "Greetings, Kezi." I put my fist to my forehead.

She bows her head. "Greetings, Olus."

We stand awkwardly, smiling but not speaking. Now that we're together I have no idea how to start. I say, "Er . . ."

She says, "Um . . ."

We laugh.

I collect myself. "You're looking for something in the market?" This isn't what I want to say.

She holds up the yarn and laughs. "Wool." Her eyes go to the wool in my basket. "Does the wool come from your goats? Do they have gold in their coats?"

I shake my head. "The wool is from Akka." I take a knife from the pouch at my waist and cut lengths from a few balls of yarn. "Here." I give them to her, samples of Enshi Rock's finest.

"Thank you." She arranges the strands in her palm.

"Kezi . . ." I may never have another chance to be alone with her. "Kezi, I know about your pado's oath. I know you're to be sacrificed."

To my astonishment, she nods. "Admat sent —"

Screams come from the market.

26
KEZI

Smoke rises above the gate lion's head. Olus drops his wool basket. He grasps my arm and we run toward the market.

A stiff wind hurries us along. I fear that the wind will fan the flames, but it dies when we get close. We race around the edges of the stalls. Although the smoke is thick, Olus seems to know where to go.

The timbrel player shrieks as he rolls on the ground, afire. Flames shoot up from the meat brazier. A woman slaps at her burning sleeve. The cook's straw cushion and several baskets are on fire. My feet dance up and down. I don't know how to help. Flame creeps up a bamboo awning pole. If the awnings catch, the whole market will go.

Liquid pours down on the pole and the cushion and the baskets. I look up. The plum-juice vat is in the air above us, dumping its contents.

The water trough flies above the burning musician. It tilts. His garments sputter and hiss.

The fire is out. I look for Olus and see him rolling a length of carpet around the arm of the woman with the burning sleeve. He seems to be concentrating only on her, but I know better. This masma saved everyone.

A wind blows the juice vat and the trough away from the market onto the King's Road, where they clatter down harmlessly.

Someone cries, "A miracle!"

A woman shouts, "Admat saved us!"

A man's voice rises, singing,

"Merciful Admat,
Who loves his people
More than he loves
His righteous fire."

Many voices chant, "Thanks to Admat."

I chant too, but I also think, Thanks to Olus, Admat's masma.

Pazur runs to me. "Mistress! You are safe!"

"And you?" I ask. There is soot in his hair. I notice ashes drifting down, soot in everyone's hair.

"I am well. We should go home now."

People are chattering to each other. No

one has heard of such a marvel as has just taken place.

"I haven't finished," I say. "Mati knows I'll be here all day." I start for the weavers' stalls. As I walk, I stuff my ball of golden wool into my tapestry sack.

Pazur follows me to a rug stall, where I go to a pile of carpets. I study the top one carefully, then lift it off and study the next. The workmanship isn't as good as mine, but I pretend to be interested.

Around me the market is settling into its ordinary state. Vendors resume their cries. Even the timbrels and drum begin again.

Pazur sits on a low stack of carpets. In a few minutes his eyes close. His head lolls sideways against an awning pole. I move to the next stall, where a merchant displays his yarns.

"You won't find wool as fine as mine here."

Olus is at my side. He has his wool basket again.

"I want to see your yarn in the light." I lead him past the sleeping Pazur, through the market aisle, and out into the sunshine.

We walk several yards until we are beyond earshot of the shoppers but still in plain sight.

"Olus, can you fly?"

"No, but I can ride my winds."

His winds?

"I can lift you, too. Would you like to ride my winds?"

I would like to ride *Admat's* winds. I nod eagerly.

"Would you like to visit Akka?"

I could live a full span of years and never see more than Hyte. "Yes, I would like to see Akka." But I can't simply go. "Wait. I'll be just a minute."

I run back to Pazur. "Wake up!"

His eyes open. "I'm awake, Mistress. I wasn't asleep."

"Pazur . . ." I don't know how long I'll be gone. "Tell Pado and Mati I'll return — at the latest — when all the figs are ripe."

He jumps up and seizes my arm.

I pull away. "Don't touch me!"

He drops his hand.

"Tell Pado and Mati about the miracle here. Tell them I've seen a sign."

His mouth drops open. I leave him. In a moment I am with Olus again. "Where is Akka?"

"In the north. Beyond the hills."

Will everyone see us fly?

Clouds blow in and cover the sun. This masma is powerful! Thick fog covers the King's Road and the market.

117

"Ready, Kezi?"

"Yes!"

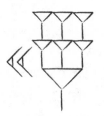

27
OLUS

"I must hold you or you'll fall."

Being held seems to her more dangerous than flying, or more against propriety. She looks away from me, then back, searching my face. I don't know whether I should smile or speak, but I do neither. Discover what you will, I think.

"Then hold me." Her face is pink.

I send my wool basket sailing to my pasture, where my herding wind is minding my goats. I touch Kezi's shoulder, then cradle her in my arms. My strong wind lifts us. My wet wind drags some fog along for concealment.

I wonder what she's guessed about me. After the fire in the market, her hopes may be too high.

We rise slowly. Her cheek is against my

chest. I can hardly think. I recite into her hair:

"Evergreen Akka,
Where the gazelle races the tiger
And where the rivers
Splash ribbons of foam
On the gray-maned mare
And her foal."

Kezi, I think, addressing her in my mind, love Akka. Love me. What I will tell you will seem impossible. Believe anyway. Do what I say to save yourself, to save us both.

My quick wind increases our pace. When we are far enough from Hyte, I disperse the fog.

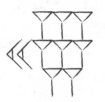

28
KEZI

Dizzy with flight and the nearness of Olus, I shut my eyes, then open them. I don't want to miss anything.

How much closer to Admat's sun are we? An eagle flies by, not far above us.

Air streams across me. I feel a mighty swell of wind beneath me. My left arm is pressed against Olus, but I put out my right with my palm open to catch more of the wind. I spread my toes in my sandals and wish my feet were bare.

I'd love to see Hyte from the sky, but positioned as I am, I can only look up and out. "Olus?"

He says something.

"What?" I shout.

"Don't be afraid," he shouts back.

"May I look down at Hyte?"

He turns me so my back is to him. I am

tilted downward. We are stretched out against each other. I gulp in the rushing air and try to ignore the feel of him.

Hyte is just a thick smudge on the horizon, but the stepped outline of the temple is clear. I can even make out the triangle of the ramp that leads to the sanctuary.

The wind lifts us higher. The temple shrinks to a dot and the city to a shadow. When they disappear entirely, Olus turns me so I am facing in the direction of our flight.

I think, My love is thoughtful.

My love? Yes, my love.

I love the hairs on Olus's arm that catch the morning sun.

Admat, is this when you send me love, before I'm to die?

The low hills around Hyte are brown, speckled with green dots of shrubs and date palms.

As we fly higher, the hills rise too. After a while I grow hungry. The morning is passing. The morning of my twenty-seventh remaining day, if I'm still to die.

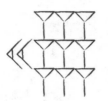

29
OLUS

The air chills. I wrap us in a cocoon of my summer wind.

"Please don't."

I take the cocoon away but fly lower. Although she may not care, I don't want her to suffer the acute cold. We are nearing my first destination, where I will tell her everything.

Here we are. I fly over it.

"Wait!" she cries. "Go back. It's . . ." She turns her head, and I see her excited face. "It's impossible!"

We circle. "Do you like it?" I'm grinning. This is what I hoped for.

"It's miraculous!"

"Does that mean you like it?"

"Very much."

We circle three times. Then my gentle wind deposits us in a meadow a few yards from the base. "This is a waterfall, the falls of Zago. We're on the border of Hyte and Akka. The Zago River flows through Akka."

From Enshi Rock, Hannu and Arduk can see us here. All the gods can if they like.

Kezi runs to the riverbank. In a moment she is wet with spray. Laughing, she sticks out her tongue to taste the water. Then she pulls off her sandals and steps delicately onto the closest wet rock. She dances from rock to rock to the ledge behind the curtain of water.

"Everything is wavery!" she cries. "You should see it."

I hesitate, although the ledge is hardly confining. Only water will separate me from open air.

"Come, my love!"

Love? Her love! Of course I join her.

In the dim light her face glows. She is blushing and her hand is over her mouth, but she doesn't take back the words. Although I'm uneasy in the small space, I lift away her hand and kiss her. I taste the water on her lips. Afterward she clings to me, a closeness I don't mind at all.

"What do you think?" She gestures at the water.

"Very wavery, my love." I don't want her to be alone in saying *my love*.

She slides out of my arms and spreads her arms to embrace the rock wall. "I like Akka."

This is not my favorite spot.

"Look!" She has found a narrow opening that leads into a cave.

I watch as she slips through the fissure. I imagine myself being trapped inside, the fissure closing.

After a minute she emerges. "There's enough room for us both. In the cave, the falls boom. Do you want to hear it?"

"No!"

"Oh!"

I fly my quick wind back onto the grass, ashamed at the relief I feel.

After a short while she joins me. She gestures and asks, "Are these mountains?"

"Foothills. The mountains aren't far."

"Olus! If these are the feet, how tall are the mountains?" Before I can answer, she sinks to her knees and runs her hands through the grass. "Smooth! Hyte grass is spiky." She stands. "Was there something dangerous in the cave?"

"No." I'm embarrassed to tell her about my fear.

She takes a deep breath. "I've never met a masma before."

"I'm not a masma."

"Please forgive me." She touches my arm.

"I was taught that masmas are evil, but you're good. I think you're Admat's masma."

I decide to confess. "I was afraid to go in the cave. Small spaces frighten me."

She smiles. "I used to be afraid of pigeons."

I smile back. "Why?"

"Their red eyes. I thought they killed people at night."

"How did you stop fearing them?"

"I don't remember." Her smile fades. "Now I'm afraid of the priest's knife."

It is time. "I'm truly not a masma. I'm the Akkan god of the winds."

30
KEZI

"Don't say that!" I want to run back into the cave for safety, although my love has boasted all safety away.

A minute passes. The sky is still blue. The forest that climbs the feet hills does not catch fire. Olus is not covered with boils.

He shouts, "I am the Akkan god of the winds."

I shout, too. "Admat, you are the one, the all."

"What can I show her?" he says to himself.

"Don't show me anything."

Two large rocks bounce out of the forest, coming toward us. Admat's punishment! I throw myself on the ground.

My bones are not crushed. I hear two thuds and raise my head. The rocks are planted in the ground, side by side.

"My clever wind found them. See? They're both chair shaped." He sits in one.

The one he's in is narrower than the other

and has a more sloping chair back. Each is chest high with a lower shelf for sitting.

"See how my clever wind —"

"Admat's wind."

"See how it placed them to face the falls."

I stand, but I don't go near the chair rocks.

"Kezi, I have just one power, the winds. But I'm immortal, and I can see and hear and detect scents at great distances. All the Akkan gods can. My love, believe me."

"If you can see so far, what is my pado doing?"

"I can't see as far as the city from here."

If not for the oath, Pado would be in his counting room, but I don't know where he is now. If not for the oath, Mati would be at her loom. Aunt Fedo would have come to gossip. Nia is probably praying. Flies buzz in the kitchen. Pado and Mati think I'm still at the market, unless Pazur has already told them I'm gone.

"Kezi, my love, what if you could become immortal?"

Admat, don't listen to this crazy masma! Forgive him! But *I* listen.

"Cala became immortal seven hundred years ago. She's the goddess of wild and domesticated animals."

Is there some masma spell to live forever? "How old are you?"

"My mati is six thousand years old. My pado is four thousand."

"And you?"

He shifts from one hip to the other in the stone chair. "Seventeen."

I can't help laughing, although I'm disappointed. Giggling, I say, "Your parents are having children at their age?"

"Seventeen years ago they did." He laughs too.

"But" — I want to show him how impossible his claim is — "before you were born, who had power over the winds?"

"Nin, the storm goddess, commanded them, but sometimes they were unruly. They always do what I tell them. Kezi, believe me. I'm a god. I have numberless years ahead."

"Olus . . . we can die anytime." Knowing when death will arrive may be better than believing it will never arrive at all. "You may live many more years, but you will die when Admat wishes. It's true!"

Instead of answering, he says, "Are you hungry?"

There is no food here. I nod and wait for more magic.

From the pouch on his belt he takes out a wedge of goat cheese. He breaks off a generous portion and gives it to me.

"Thank you." I take it and touch the empty stone chair. It is solid, warmed by the sun. I dare sit in it, although I brace myself for it to explode.

He takes a piece of cheese for himself and begins to eat.

"Mmm!" I say, tasting the cheese.

He pulls a puffy brown loaf from the pouch. By its smooth crust I can tell that it is not a meat and barley loaf. With the knife he used before on his wool, he cuts a slice for me.

It's pale tan inside. I smell rye, caraway, and a scent I can't identify. I take a bite.

The slice tastes like bread, but it feels much softer — cloud pudding. "What is it? It's delicious!" This *is* magic.

"Leavened bread. In Hyte you have only flatbread."

We eat. Sitting there, he appears to be an ordinary — extraordinarily handsome — person. No one could tell he's a masma. I know how kind he is, and I know I love him. I should leave the rest to Admat.

"Kezi . . . I am immortal, whether you think so or not. But I don't know if you can be. It isn't simple."

If he had said it was simple, I would have known it wasn't possible. "Olus, if an immortal" — I refuse to say *god* — "were sacrificed, what would happen?"

"The priest's knife would hurt, but the immortal would recover. Your pado would fulfill his oath, but you would live."

Admat, forgive me. "How does a mortal become immortal?"

31
OLUS

Before answering her question, I say, "If you were immortal, we could build a house here."

Her eyes shift away from me.

I've said something wrong. "Are you angry?"

She shakes her head.

"First we would do the wedding pantomime, and nothing would pull us apart."

She's crying. I'm at her side, bending over her, taking her hands.

She leans her head against my chest. "You haven't" — she grasps my waist and looks up — "even asked about my dowry."

"The dowry doesn't matter." I wipe her tears.

She laughs a wet laugh. "It would be a big dowry. But I want to live in Hyte."

"We can live in Hyte."

"I would still worship Admat."

"I know."

"It would be his will if I became immortal."

I nod.

"Now tell me."

I kneel at her knees. "First we have to go to Enshi Rock, but I don't know if we can."

"Is Enshi Rock in Akka?"

"Yes, but it's over Akka. It floats in the sky."

"Mmm. Why did you leave?"

"I was lonely." She won't believe this either: "No one but me is young."

"Are your parents still there?"

"Yes. Kezi, only a god or a mortal hero or heroine can reach Enshi Rock. I think you're a heroine —"

"I'm not!"

"You saved your aunt. I think that's heroism. But it may not be enough."

"If I'm not a heroine?"

"You'll have to perform an act of heroism. I don't know what."

"Go on."

"Once you are a heroine, you can go to Enshi Rock with a champion."

She touches my chin. "You."

I stand. "I don't think I'm a champion."

She jumps out of her chair rock. "You rescued me from Elon and saved everyone at the market!"

133

I smile at her vehemence. "If I'm not a champion, I'll have to become one."

"How?"

"I don't know that either. Some kind of trial."

"What happens when we arrive on Enshi Rock, if we can?"

"You have . . . you have . . ." My voice is gone. I swallow and try again. "It's . . ."

"Yes?"

"I can't say. The words won't come out. There's an act you must perform to become immortal, a pleasant act, but Cala alone has ever succeeded at it."

"I wish an altar were here." She kneels. "Admat, please do not make me die so soon. Let me become a heroine. Let me succeed at the masmas' test. As you wish, so it will be."

Feeling ridiculous to be praying to another god, I echo, "As you wish, so it will be."

"How do we find out if I'm a heroine and you're a champion?"

"We try to go to Enshi Rock." I hold my arms out for her, and she nestles into them.

My swift wind carries us. Two hours pass. We start up the lower slope of Mount Enshi and pass high above a hamlet. Three men are building a hut next to a freshly dug well. Someone must be betrothed. I recognize

Kudiya, the boy — young man now — who thought I was a vision. He may be the groom. Kudiya, I think, I have my bride, too.

32
KEZI

The mountains we've been flying among are tall. Now we are halfway up the grandest of them, its heights wreathed in clouds.

"This is Mount Enshi," Olus shouts. "Above it is Enshi Rock. I'll clear the sky so you can see."

Olus does his masma wind magic, and the clouds blow away. The mountain ends in the rounded mouth of a volcano. Above the volcano — *above* it! My fingers dig into Olus's arm. Above the volcano, ivory and topaz cliffs rise in vertical shafts.

Enshi Rock floats in the sky.

I squeeze my eyes shut and open them. The rock is still floating. This is beyond a masma's spell. Olus *is* a god!

I stiffen against him.

"There's nothing to fear," he shouts, holding me tighter.

I fear *him,* the god Olus.

Clouds return and hide the rock again.

Olus mutters something. I crane my neck to see his face. He's frowning. Is his wrath directed at me? Have I done something to offend him?

He says into my hair, "We're almost there, my love."

He isn't angry at me.

We fly up Mount Enshi. I try to shrink into myself to create distance from him.

I want to pray, but to whom?

Fog curls around us. The wind that carries us slows. We hang in the clouds. I understand that we can't rise farther.

He says, "I must not be a champion."

How can a god not be a champion? I must not be a heroine.

As soon as we begin to descend, Olus's winds are free again. We land on the lip of the volcano. I stumble away from him. "Forgive me . . . forgive me. . . ." I want to hide from his presence.

"Kezi! What is it?"

There's nowhere to hide. There are only ashes and shiny black stones.

"Kezi!" He runs after me.

I can't outrun a god. I throw myself on the rough ground.

"Don't!" he yells. "Stand up!"

I stand.

"Look at me."

I can't meet his eyes. I stare a little to the side, as one does with Admat's altar flame.

"Don't worship me," he begs. "I'm only Olus."

No, he's not. I begin to weep. Bending over, I sob and sink to my knees. I can't help it, even though he commanded me to stand.

How can Admat be the one, the all, if Olus is a god too and there are many Akkan gods?

Admat is angry at the people of Hyte sometimes, but he loves us. Doesn't he? He is with us every moment. Isn't he? He is with me every moment.

Isn't he?

Is he nowhere and nothing?

Am I alone?

33
OLUS

Kezi raises her head. Tears drip from the tip of her nose. "Olus, god of the winds, forgive —"

"Stop!" I take her hand, which is limp in mine, an obedient, worshipful hand. "Kezi . . ." I raise her up and move her hand to my chest. "Do you feel my heart?"

She nods. The tears course down her cheeks.

I let her hand go, and it drops like the hand of a puppet. I pull around us my comforting breeze, which carries the scent of cypress.

Gradually she stops crying. "Olus, god of the winds, forgive my —"

"There's no need for forgiveness."

She looks up, where Enshi Rock is again hidden by clouds. "Olus, god of the winds, is there a god above the Akkan gods, one you pray to?"

I wish she'd stop saying *god of the winds*.

"We don't pray. Ursag — he's the god of wisdom — believes more may exist than we know. The *more* may be Admat. Most of his holy text may be true."

She whispers, "But Admat is not the one, the all."

"No."

"Olus, god of the winds, did you make the altar flame flare when Pado swore his oath?"

"I didn't cause the flare. Admat may have, or something else. The lamp oil may have been impure."

The earth rumbles and growls. The ground tilts. Instantly we are ankle deep in stones and ash.

"Admat!" Kezi shouts.

I lift her, ready to ride a wind to safety. She is wood in my arms. The ground levels as the world rights itself. I set her down. She backs away from me.

"It was just Hannu. My mati. She probably doesn't like one of her pots. When she's annoyed, she isn't careful."

"She's the goddess of pottery?"

"Of pottery and of the earth."

"The earth!" She faces away from me. "Olus, god of the winds . . . forgive me. I'm just someone who likes to dance and knot pretty rugs. I can't become a goddess."

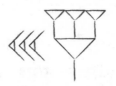

34
KEZI

"Kezi, we have no holy text."

Without turning, I know his eyes are pleading. How can a god be pleading with me? How can I know a god so well?

"We're not everywhere and everything. My knowledge is different from yours, but no greater. I'm a clumsy dancer. I don't know how to make rugs. If the ground were smoother, I would kneel to you."

I shake my head so hard, it hurts.

"I *should* kneel. It takes more courage to be a mortal than it takes to be a god."

"Olus" — I use all my own courage to ask this — "god of the winds, have you ever killed any mortals?"

"No! And none have been sacrificed to me. We don't allow it."

"Olus, god of the winds, have you punished any mortals?"

"Elon."

I hear the satisfaction in his voice. My fear lessens — a little.

"But Elon suffered no more than a scraped knee and a bump on his head. Oh! Once I punished a merchant by stealing his spices."

Not a terrible punishment. "Why, Olus, god of the winds?"

"First his camel kicked me, and then he kicked me. Elon kicked me, too. Remember? People seem to like to kick me."

I can't help smiling.

"I wish *you* would kick me instead of being afraid of me."

I turn around.

He turns too and presents his rump. "Kick me."

"Oh, Olus." I'm laughing, and I forget to call him *god of the winds.* "I can't kick you." He's become Olus the masma again to me, even though I know he's a god. "I don't want to kick you."

He faces me. When I meet his gaze, at first I see worry in his eyes. Then his whole face smiles, as if I were the god and I had stopped being angry at him. He holds out his right hand. I hesitate. Should I?

I take his hand and raise it above my head. Dip, step, dip, step. Low kick. I come in close for a kiss. He smells of the waterfall.

He kisses me again. And again.

We pull apart a little but remain so close, our breaths mingle.

"Love, do you still believe in Admat?"

"How can I tell?"

He brushes ash from the neckline of my tunic. "Must you be sacrificed?"

Must I? "If I'm not, Admat — if he exists — will punish me and Pado and Mati and my children and grandchildren." He may even be able to punish Olus.

"Worse than death?" He adds quickly, "I know there are worse punishments."

And many ways to die more painful than by a priest's knife. "My family still believes." I walk to the edge of the volcano. My twenty-seventh day is ending. I can barely see the lava steam below.

If I'm sacrificed after I become immortal, will I endanger Pado or Mati? Becoming a goddess has nothing to do with them. Pado will have fulfilled his oath. "I can live only if I'm immortal."

Olus sounds sad. "Don't you want to be immortal?"

"To save my life, yes. To live forever . . . I can't imagine how that would be."

"Neither can I."

I turn my back on the volcano. "But you

know how it is for the other gods."

"A few have put themselves to endless sleep, but not the rest." He comes and tugs me gently away from the edge. "You might step off without realizing. My winds can't go into the volcano."

He's such a loving person . . . masma . . . god!

"Olus, I'd rather live a human life — worship a god, have a husband and children and grandchildren, knot many rugs, and die."

"I might, too. Er . . . I don't mean have a husband or knot a rug."

We laugh.

I say, "I'm not a heroine, so —"

"You are! I'm not a champion."

"You are, or neither of us is. What must we do?"

"The god of wisdom will know. I'll go to Enshi Rock and ask him."

I have to stay here alone!

"Don't worry. We'll descend to the lower slopes. You can wait for me there."

"Olus . . ." I'm frightened again. How did he know I didn't want to be here by myself? "Can you read minds or hear my thoughts?"

"No." He drops his arm and steps away from me. "You did this." He hitches up his shoulders. "You did it with Elon too.

Come." He holds out his arms to carry me.

"Might I ride a wind on my own?"

Oh! I'm in the air! I'm sliding — very fast. My legs are higher than my head. I wave my arms, trying to right myself. Next to me Olus is laughing! His wind raises my back and head. I'm still sliding but sitting up. Amazing!

We zoom down the mountain, a few feet from the ground. The tree line is rushing at us. We'll crash!

My wind lifts me, and his does the same. We're inches above the trees. I reach down. My wind slows while I run my hand through leaves. Then the wind gains speed again.

A few minutes later we are received by the soft Akkan grass on a stream bank.

"This is better. Can you stay here?"

I nod. Olus gives me the rest of the cheese.

A breeze brushes across my arms. "I smell roses! And cheese."

"My stalwart wind loves roses. If there's danger, it will carry you to safety."

"Hurry back."

"I'll return as soon as I see Ursag. If I have to undergo a trial, I'll tell you." He kisses me. Then one of his winds takes him. He rises, facing me, peering down until his head disappears into a cloud. It swallows the rest of him, but I continue to look up, hoping the cloud will float away. After a few minutes it does. I see a black speck, then only blue.

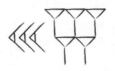

35
OLUS

The sky has cleared and the early stars have come out when I reach our temple, which sits high on four thick stone legs, like table legs. Hannu created the temple to be open to the air at its base, as if she knew she'd someday have a son who feared tight places. The temple stairs twist around the eastern stone leg and enter the temple at the first story. I begin to climb. Ursag's library takes up the entire fifth story.

I'm halfway to the door at the top of the stairs when Puru appears three steps above me.

He may know what needs to be done better than Ursag. I say, "Kezi —"

"I . . . will . . . go . . . to her."

"Why? Wait!" The sight of him will frighten her. But Puru has vanished. Although I jump on my swift wind, I can never catch up, because Puru's travel is instantaneous. As I skim off Enshi Rock, I look down to see her. There she is, on the stream bank, still alone. Puru must have gone somewhere else first. Perhaps I can reach her before he does.

My swift wind carries me into a thunder-cloud, as it has many times. I'll be beyond the cloud in a moment. But the cloud changes into a swarm of bees. How could it?

Although I flail my arms, the bees stay with me, buzzing and stinging. I've been stung before, but not like this. I close my eyes to protect my eyeballs. My wind carries the bees with me. I summon my whisking wind, but it can't whisk them free.

My skin burns, tightens, presses in on me. I am as squeezed and swollen as a blister. I scream. My howling wind joins in, the yowl streaming behind me but not drowning out the furious bees.

The buzzing and stinging stop. I squint down at myself between bloated eyelids. My throat is raw from screaming. The bees are growing, flattening, changing —

Into spiders! Hundreds of spiders! I swipe at them, but they cling. My whisking wind fails again. The spiders are spinning thick webs across me. My voice is silenced as threads cross my mouth.

In my terror, I lose command of my swift wind. I'm spiraling I don't know where.

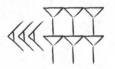

36
KEZI

Night falls. I sit on the stream bank, knees drawn up to my chest for warmth. Olus's stalwart wind surrounds me, although there seems to be no danger. After a while I curl on my side, listen to the water, and close my mind to the future.

Birdsong wakes me. The call of one bird is *twee-tee-twit,* sounding in my ears like *twenty-six twenty-six twenty-six,* over and over, numbering my remaining days.

Olus should have returned by now.

The sun has warmed me. I drink from the icy stream. My teeth ache, but the water is delicious. A breeze rustles through the canopy of leaves in the woods behind me. Olus's breeze. I wonder if he sent it to tell me he's on his way. His stalwart wind still curls around me. I know by the roses.

I'm hungry. A few yards downstream is a plum tree loaded with fruit. Pushing worry away — about Olus, about me — I dance to the tree. When I shake the trunk, breakfast rains down. I crouch and collect plums in the lap of my tunic.

The stream parts around a wide flat rock. Holding my tunic out, I step stones to reach it. On the rock I sit and eat, dropping pits in the water. When I'm finished, I take Olus's ball of wool out of my waist sack. I wind one end a few turns around my finger.

The birdsong ceases.

"Kezi . . ."

I jump up. Olus's wool falls into the stream and is carried away.

A man wrapped in orange linen stands under the plum tree. Is he a man or only man shaped? Is there flesh under the cloth?

Olus's stalwart wind should take me out of danger, but it does nothing.

"I . . . won't . . . hurt . . . you."

If a desert could speak, it would have his voice.

Might this be Admat, the cloth covering his invisibility?

Toes and the top of a sandal peep out from under the lowest linen strip. Five ordinary-seeming toes and toenails give me enough confidence to stammer, "W-who are y-you?" I bow my head, then raise it to watch him.

"I've . . . come . . . to . . . help you find your destiny. Perhaps you can become a heroine."

His accent is the same as Olus's. I hear *helb* and *berhabs*.

"I . . . am . . . Puru. . . ."

Buru is probably Puru. I wonder if he's another Akkan god or a true masma, an evil one, making himself sound Akkan. I hop stones to the opposite bank. "Did the god of the winds send you?"

"The . . . god . . . of . . . fate does no one's bidding." He vanishes and reappears at my side.

Aa! I back away. A branch cracks under my foot.

He advances.

"Olus will return soon," I say. And blow you away.

A raspy chuckle. "Not . . . soon. . . ."

Olus! "Why not?"

"He . . . is . . . undergoing . . . his trial for you."

"To become a champion?"

Another chuckle and no answer.

Olus will be safe. He's a god! But I'm frightened for both of us.

If this Puru is lying, Olus will come.

"Olus . . . doesn't . . . know . . . how you can reach Enshi Rock, but I do."

"You can help me?"

Puru's head swivels from side to side. "No . . . one . . . can . . . help you, but I can tell you how to attempt it."

"How?"

"You . . . must . . . go . . . beneath the volcano."

"I want to go up, not down."

"You . . . may . . . rise . . ." His linen finger points up. ". . . only by descending." The finger points down.

I wish I could see his face.

"You . . . must . . . go . . . to Wadir, to the world of the warkis."

"I'll be dead soon enough!"

"If . . . you . . . seek . . . immortality, you must visit Wadir."

But Wadir is in the west, not under a volcano — or so I was taught.

"Come." He walks into the woods.

I don't know what to do. Olus! Admat! Olus! I don't move.

He turns. "I . . . can . . . leave . . . you. It is of little importance to me. You must decide." He waits.

A bunting perches on his head, raises its pale throat, and sings. The bird isn't afraid of him.

"I'm coming." I can stop at any time, and I don't have to do what he tells me to.

He's on a narrow path. I follow several paces behind. He sets his feet with care, seemingly unaccustomed to walking. The linen, which is skirtlike down to his knees, shortens his steps.

We walk for hours. The rhythm of our slow march and the scent of roses put me into a trance. The moon rises. My twenty-sixth day has slipped away.

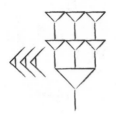

37
OLUS

I careen through the air trussed in spider thread. My slitted eyes peer from the gray web into the night sky. I call on my winds, but my commands are wrapped inside with me.

Threads circle my throat, pressing into my windpipe. I suck in air between my teeth.

My fingernails scratch the webbing on my hands. These spiders spin with ropes of iron! I continue to scratch. My fingers curl. My nails cut into my palms. Spiders spin my chin to my chest. Mount Enshi is below.

My stomach lurches. I am dropping, plummeting. I crash down. Hear a splash. Feel pain slam through my back. My upper and lower teeth clack against each other. My eyes descend into their sockets.

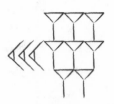

38
KEZI

Puru stops. I bump into him and leap back.
In the moonlight I see his hand circle the
thin trunk of a mulberry bush. He pulls.
The bush, its roots, and the earth around
them come up easily.

A tunnel is revealed. Rough rock stairs
descend into the mountain. Beyond the top
few steps the darkness is complete.

Puru yanks a branch off the mulberry and
raises it toward the night sky. A star deepens
to orange. The branch begins to burn,
brightly at first. Then it dims but doesn't go
out.

"Your . . . torch . . . will . . . give light
until you reach Wadir. Olus's wind will
depart as soon as you enter the tunnel. It
cannot flow underground. If Olus follows
you to Wadir, he will lose his powers and no
longer be a god. He'll be mortal, like you."

"He mustn't follow me!"

Puru thrusts the glowing branch into the ground.

"Are there gods who are still gods in the underworld? Is Admat there?"

"I . . . have . . . never . . . been to Wadir. When you arrive, you must pluck a feather from a warki."

The warkis have wings? Under a mountain?

"The . . . feather . . . is . . . essential. Pluck it quickly. Do nothing else. Eat nothing. Drink nothing. The warkis will want to keep you. If you remain long enough to sprout feathers, you'll be there forever."

"Why are you telling me this?"

His voice becomes even raspier. I can barely make out his words.

"Fate . . . may . . . be . . . thwarted." He's silent. Then, "I . . . long . . . for . . . a happy outcome."

I'm not sure I heard him correctly. "Please, Puru, did you say . . ."

He's vanished.

I sit down with my back to a tree, several feet from the tunnel mouth. I picture the warkis as skeletons with wings and try not to imagine becoming one of them.

Eventually I fall asleep. In my dream Mati bends over her loom. Pado counts the servants' wages. Nia sits outside our door. Aunt Fedo approaches her, while the asupu scatters dead mice up and down the street.

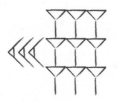

39
OLUS

I awaken to smarting skin. My back is soaked. Some liquid must have seeped into the spiderweb. My knees are folded against my chest. I hear the slap of water against . . . a riverbank? Kezi's stream bank?

The water is a few inches deep. I open my eyes. The lids are less swollen. It's still night or night again or dark as night.

"Kezi?" My voice is muffled, but the webbing across my mouth has loosened.

No answer.

Fear tightens around me.

I call for my soothing wind, but it doesn't come. I call for my mighty wind, but it doesn't come. Come! Any wind!

My god's power has deserted me. Bound, and I have nothing.

How much time has elapsed? Might Kezi's

month have passed? Is she — Will I never —

My hands are spun into fists, but the spiders are gone. Perhaps their departure loosened the threads. I straighten my fingers, pushing against the resistance of the web. I scratch at my left forearm. My nails break through the webbing and expose a little skin. Frantically I scratch. My fingers stick to my arm. Muscles straining, I pull my fingers away, trailing strands that thin and finally snap.

Someone groans — a deep, male groan. A man is curled next to me. There may be others. What horror have I landed in? I peer around.

I'm in a well! In a spiderweb in a well.

I am panting. I close my eyes and imagine the sky.

My winds haven't deserted me. They can't come underground. If I can climb out, they will be mine again.

I open my eyes and scratch the webbing again, gritting my teeth, making myself be patient.

The man moans. I see that he and I are alone here. I can do nothing for him unless I am free. Eventually I peel the spider threads from everywhere I can reach. They clump into sticky gobs that I shake into the water, where they sink and then bob to the surface.

The man wheezes. I turn to him and wince. My back hurts!

The man's hair is bloody, his eyes closed, his left ear and cheek submerged.

I know him. He is Kudiya, whom I last saw building a hut near a new well.

We're in the new well! Could this be my trial to be Kezi's champion? Is saving Kudiya what I must do?

The rocks that line the well are wet. Water is trickling in. Tiny rivulets stream downward.

I pray the well was built with care. If not, it could collapse and bury us. I picture the rocks working loose, crashing down.

I close my eyes until I am calmer. Then I pull Kudiya onto my lap and rinse the cut on his head. The blood continues to flow.

He'll die. The well will cave in. I'll be immured with his corpse.

His eyelids flutter. I don't know what light he's seeing by, but he gets out, "Olus . . . my . . . vision."

"Can you stand?"

He shakes his head. "Leg."

I raise his tunic. His right knee is twice the size of his left. It must be broken. He won't be able to climb out.

"Help!" I shout, tilting my head up. Someone can throw us a rope. We'll be saved! My voice echoes against the rocks. "Help!"

He coughs. "Gone. . . . Baby." He huffs out the story. A child has been born in this hamlet's brother village. Everyone has gone to celebrate. They will be away for days.

The well wall seems to pulse. I imagine pythons oozing between the rocks, winding around me, squeezing me.

I find something nearby to stare at, something not frightening, an inch of Kudiya's threadbare tunic. The wall is not pulsing. There will be no pythons.

"Fly . . . me. . . ." Kudiya smiles. "God . . . winds."

"I'll have to carry you." I support him as I stand. He's twig skinny and shorter than I am. The water reaches our ankles.

Ah! The low water means that not very much time has passed since Kezi and I flew over. Her month isn't over. Somewhere she's still alive.

I arrange Kudiya's arms around my neck. "Hang on."

He hugs me as tight as the spiderwebs, tight as a python, strangling me. He's turned into a python!

I throw him off.

He's only Kudiya, but he's lying facedown in the water. In my madness, could I have killed him? The rocks press in on me. I sway, catch myself, spread my legs for balance. The rocks are not pressing in!

I squat to raise him. He lives! He sputters, coughs up water, and sags against me. I put his arms around my neck again. "Not so tight."

He grips me just as before. I think him a python again. I tear his arms apart, make sure they *are* arms, and keep myself from dropping him. "Not so tight!"

Better.

Between the rocks are plenty of handholds and footholds. I step out of my sandals, rise on my toes, and stretch. My fingers find their places. I will do this.

But the rocks are too wet. My fingers slip and slip again.

I put Kudiya down. His chin slumps onto his chest. His every breath is a gasp. He won't last long without aid from someone who knows how to staunch his bleeding and set his leg.

I shift my position. The pouch at my waist brushes my hip.

My knife!

I pull it out and stab it between two rocks over my head. It holds my weight. Can I grip the rocks with my fingers and toes for long enough to move the knife? I can!

I hang Kudiya's arms around my neck and insert the knife again. Instantly the drag of him on my shoulders pulls it out. I try a narrower space with the same result. Another attempt. Another failure.

Over and over I stab the rock wall.

40
KEZI

In the morning I awaken with a dry mouth and gnawing hunger.

The sky is clear. Above is Enshi Rock, and next to it — much smaller — is the daytime three-quarter moon.

I wonder if Olus is still undergoing his trial. It comes to me that his trial must be, or must have been, his worst fear. He would be shut in somewhere.

Could he be trapped eternally?

If he is being brave, I must be too. I approach the tunnel, then back away. First, food and water. If I mustn't eat or drink in Wadir, I shouldn't leave this world hungry.

Twenty minutes later I find a brook. I drink and drink. Tiny fish abound in the sparkling water but slip between my fingers. After half an hour I see a big carp swimming lazily my way.

Out of habit I pray, Thank you, Admat!

I catch it with my hands. It struggles, but I hang on. On the ground, it flops about as I drink again, more than I want.

While I'm with the warkis, I'll search for Admat. The holy text says he is visible in Wadir. If I find him, I'll beg him to let Pado break his oath and to send a sign that my family and Nia will understand. Only Admat can grant me an ordinary long life in Hyte with Olus.

I carry the fish to the tunnel and use the glowing branch to light a fire. When the fish is cooked, I tear into it. The morning is almost over.

Holding the branch high, I enter the tunnel. As soon as I descend a step, the scent of roses is replaced by a smell of mold. Olus's stalwart wind has wafted away.

41
OLUS

I lower Kudiya to the ground and prop his back against the rock wall. The water laps at his chest. His lips are parched. We're in a well, and he's thirsty, and I've failed to notice. I cup my hands and bring water to his mouth. He's unable to drink, but I moisten his lips.

Climbing is possible only without him. If I leave him, I won't become a champion. He'll die and Kezi will die.

Above is a coin of blue sky. Perhaps someone has noticed Kudiya's absence and has returned from the brother village. I cry out for help. No one comes.

The rock wall is pulsing again. No, it's not.

I'm certain the well is smaller than it was when I landed here. It will shrink and shrink until I am plastered against Kudiya, crushing the last life out of him.

He cries, "Mati!" and tries to stand. "Mati!"

He's delirious. I ask him anyway, because I am half delirious myself, "Kudiya, is the well closing in on us?"

Eyes wide, he looks around. He pants, "Yes."

He thinks so too!

"Mati!" he shouts.

I pace the diameter of the well, toe to heel in the water. Five feet. I pace again to be sure I counted right. The water swirls around me.

Four feet.

I pace again.

Five feet.

Four feet.

Three feet!

Five feet.

I can't stop counting.

Five feet.

Four feet.

The well is playing with me.

Five feet.

Four feet.

I need to know if the well is shrinking. It's the fact I need most.

Five feet.

My ears are drumming.

Four feet.

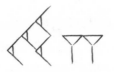

42
KEZI

Sometimes I have to crouch to continue down the stairs. Sometimes the tunnel ceiling is so high that I can't see it, not even when I raise my branch, which glows steadily. The air is cool and wet and sad. I feel I am breathing in and out sadness.

The steps are uneven. I slide my palm along the wall for balance. Keeping from falling takes most of my concentration, which may be why this realization is so slow to come: I don't know how long I've been in the tunnel. Down here there is no difference between day and night. I won't be able to count the days until my sacrifice.

But I must! I stop. My time is so precious. I have to know how much is left.

Even if I lose my chance at immortality?

Maybe. I can't think in this gloom. Carefully, I turn and try to climb back, but I can't lift my foot. It will not obey me.

Down is possible, if not easy. Up is impossible.

I begin to count the steps as a way of keeping time. Slow and cautious as each one is, five steps may fill a minute. Ten steps. Twenty-five. One hundred. Six hundred. Two hours, more or less.

One thousand steps. My legs ache. I'm hungry and thirsty again. The stairs never end. I sink down to rest but drag myself to my feet immediately. While I'm idle, there is no way to mark the time. I try to picture the blue sky, Olus's face, my home in Hyte. But the images belong to the upper air.

Two thousand steps. Above, night must have fallen. My twenty-fifth day is over. Admat, or any god who is listening, let me reach Wadir. Let me find Admat. Let me return to light and Olus.

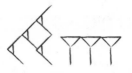

43
OLUS

Five feet.

Four feet.

I shriek, "Stop!" and stop pacing.

For a moment I'm bewildered, not sure what I've been doing. The water has risen to my thighs. It's night again. I've passed what I believe is Kezi's twenty-fifth day down here.

I lift Kudiya to make one more attempt at carrying him out. We fall and land splashing. His eyes are all whites. I prop him up so his head will stay above the water as long as possible. I begin to climb alone.

It is easier than I expect. I think the well has tipped, giving me a slope, not a vertical. Betraying Kudiya and Kezi makes everything possible.

After I emerge I will go straight to Enshi Rock and join the gods who sleep away the millennia. I won't see Kezi's sacrifice or tell

171

her good-bye or say I didn't love her enough.

I am weeping, pitying her and me.

Mostly me.

I pause, feeling supremely foolish. She'll die and Kudiya will die. I'll lose her and sleep out my own life because of fear.

I drop back down, a vertical fall again. Kudiya may die, and so may Kezi. I may sleep away eternity. But I'll stay with him until he takes his last breath.

His head is tilted back, floating as though no body were attached. I hold him up.

If I had something in addition to my knife . . . I look at the rising water where the balled-up spiderwebbing —

I grab a clump. The webbing is still sticky. I spread the mass across the fingers of my right hand. I grip a rock and can hold on despite the wet.

Am I now stuck to the rock? No. I'm able to let go. I plaster spider glue across my palms and fingers and on the undersides of my feet. It adheres even in the water. I drape Kudiya over my shoulder, where he hangs limp.

I can climb! The spider glue never fails. Soon I'll feel my winds again.

We've risen about eight feet. Above, the night sky has grown from a coin to plate.

I hear a rumble, like thunder, but this thunder is in the ground.

Hannu!

The rocks tremble.

I climb frantically. We have only a few yards to go.

The rocks dance in place.

I find new handholds, new footholds. We're almost there.

The rumble grows. The rocks slide sideways. But we're out. My strong wind lifts us above the heaving earth.

Now I have to find someone who can save Kudiya or make his dying comfortable. I command my swift wind to take us to the nearby hamlet.

But Kudiya evaporates from my arms. The ground continues to buck, then levels. The well is gone, replaced by a rock-filled basin. Next to the basin is a rubble of wood and thatch, a collapsed hut. On the ground between the two, Puru appears.

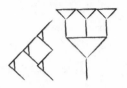

44
KEZI

The light changes so gradually that I fail to notice Puru's branch dimming and the tunnel brightening.

Three thousand steps. I lose my balance and tumble the final three, landing on my side. My fall is cushioned somehow. Still, I've made a lively arrival among the dead.

I sneeze. Gray feathers billow around me. When I stand, they're ankle deep, like ghostly fallen leaves. I brush them off and am relieved that touching them hasn't made any sprout from my skin. Puru's branch lies next to my foot, no longer glowing. I pick it up, but the light doesn't return. It's just a branch. I drop it.

By my reckoning, I was in the tunnel for ten hours. Twenty-four full days more until my sacrifice. I begin to count off seconds. One-and-two-and . . .

The chilly air stinks of decay. Glistening lava bubbles drift overhead from left to right under a rock ceiling.

Twelve-and-thirteen-and . . .

The bubbles give out a muddy light. I turn in a circle but can see only a few yards into the gloom.

Twenty-six-twenty-seven . . .

When I complete my circle, the stairway is gone. I spin around, expecting to see it somewhere, maybe gliding away from me. But it's vanished.

I was unable to climb anyway. I swallow across my parched throat.

Thirty-two-thirty-three . . .

I will search for Admat while ignoring thirst and hunger. If I find him, I will do as he wishes.

If I don't find him, I will pluck a feather from a warki. First I must meet a warki.

Forty-five-forty-six . . .

"Argenbblahemme." The voice is in the middle range, neither high nor low. A creature shuffles toward me. I suppose it is a warki. It holds a clay goblet.

The warki is no skeleton. It's plump as an ostrich, with feathers but without wings.

"Kloddaffflunghwhi."

"I seek a god called Admat, although he may have another name here."

"Plijjaffinminn."

The warki's feathers are short and gray, like those that blanket the ground. Stripped of them, it might look human. I can't tell whether it's male or female. Its feet may be webbed, taloned, or toed. They're hidden in the carpet of feathers.

It edges closer, holding the goblet out to me.

Puru says I should pluck a feather. But the feather may whisk me away, and I want to look for Admat.

I see the warki's eyes under its feathered eyebrows and between its tiny feathery lashes. Even the skin on its face is downy. It has utterly human brown eyes. Their expression is bewildered and pleading, although its mouth smiles.

The eyes awaken my pity. "How did you die? When?"

"Opoijmb." It pushes the goblet under my nose.

The liquid is violet colored. It may have an aroma, but I can't tell through the stinking air. The beverage looks poisonous, and Puru said I mustn't drink. Still, I'm so thirsty that I'm tempted. I reach out and pull my arm back — and realize I've stopped counting seconds. Losing count is worse than the tunnel, worse than the sad air or

176

the chill or the smell.

"Phndosxvtghy?"

Blinking away tears, I go around the warki and follow the floating lava bubbles. I hope they'll lead me away from the volcano and farther into Wadir. The feathers on the ground *shish-shish* as I pass. The warki with the goblet *shish-shish*es behind me.

My stomach rumbles. I see more warkis ahead, dining at a long rickety table. A narrow brook of sparkling violet liquid separates me from them. I try to jump across, but I slip on the feathers and land with my face inches above the stream. If I put out my tongue, I can catch the spray and relieve my thirst. What harm could a few drops do?

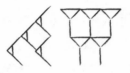

45
OLUS

"What did you do with Kudiya?" My strong wind jolts me down to face Puru, the well basin behind me.

"That . . . wasn't . . . Kudiya. . . ."

"Who was he? Where's Kudiya?"

"Kudiya . . . is . . . attending . . . the birth."

I look. There he is at a feast table in the brother village, feeding grapes to a laughing young woman. No broken leg. No bloody head. "Who was in the well?"

"A . . . vision. . . ."

"Did you create it?"

"No. . . . I . . . saw . . . it on its way. You flew into your destiny."

I saved a life that wasn't living. After the bees and the spiders, I should have guessed.

"But . . . the . . . earth . . . truly did heave."

A pig dashes by, bleating its distress. The villagers are lucky to be away.

"Where is Kezi?"

"In . . . Wadir. . . ."

Dead! Only my strong wind keeps me erect. I command it to fly me to Enshi Rock, where I will begin my long sleep. My wind lifts me.

"Becoming . . . a . . . heroine. . . ."

I drop back down. She's alive among the dead. I can't see into Wadir. None of us can.

"And . . . you . . . are . . . a champion."

Am I? I evaluate myself, searching for what's altered. In all ways I feel the same, except . . . I go to a collapsed hut and crawl into the small opening that remains. The inside reeks of sheep cheese and sweat. I feel no fear. If Kezi were at my side, I could be happy here. I squirm out. I could be happy in a walnut shell — with Kezi. Now I can bring her to Enshi Rock.

I'll go to her. "How did she reach Wadir?"

"The . . . tunnel . . . is . . . gone."

"How will she leave?"

He tells me about plucking the feather and neither eating nor drinking. The task seems simple enough.

"She . . . seeks . . . Admat . . . there. If she stays long enough to sprout her own feathers, she cannot leave."

I have to find her.

"If . . . you . . . help . . . her, she won't become a heroine. If you enter the volcano, you will not be god of the winds."

I know that. Entering the volcano means going underground.

"In . . . Wadir . . . you . . . will not be a god at all. You will be as mortal as Kezi. After a while you'll grow feathers and become a warki. Then you'll never leave."

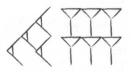

46
KEZI

I press my lips together and don't drink from the brook. On my second try I leap across without falling. The warki splashes through behind me. We approach the warkis who are dining. When we're close, I see their food is mud. Yet they eat with gusto, dipping bone spoons into bowls of mud soup, gnawing on mud drumsticks, and devouring mud flatbread. A warki offers me a plate of mud chops.

Is it spiced mud? Is there any goodness in it? I'm so hungry! I turn away.

I leave the diners and continue to follow the lava bubbles. Holding its goblet, the warki — my warki, as I've begun to think of it — accompanies me to a cooking area. A warki stirs mud in a cauldron. Another hefts a mud pig shape into a clay oven. As they work, they jabber at each other.

From the strange kitchen my warki and I

walk past a washer warki who dumps a sack of feathers into a vat of boiling violet liquid. A jeweler warki rolls mud into beads. A dilapidated rug loom stands idle. Next to the loom is a basket of feathers.

A potter warki coils mud into plates, just as potters do in Hyte. This seems ordinary and reasonable, so I speak. "Is Admat here? Can you direct me to him?"

"Lomiknbju."

Beyond the potter, pairs of warkis perform a hopping dance, holding hands, leaning into each other and then away. They roll their hips and shake their shoulders.

I can't help stopping to watch, although I shouldn't delay. The dancers are awkward but enthusiastic. How odd that there's no music. Yet they keep perfect time with one another.

My warki never stops smiling in spite of its sad eyes and the gloom that's so thick in the air, I can almost eat it.

I keep checking my arms and legs to be sure I haven't sprouted a feather.

We enter a forest of dead pistachio trees. Dry, brown leaves and bunches of blackened fruit cling to the branches. Light from the lava bubbles barely seeps into the forest. A bubble touches a high branch and bursts. Drops of lava fall on the leaves. One drop lands on my hand, a warm splash.

The trees thin. I glimpse a shining building in the distance. A clearing opens. The building is a copper temple, no taller than I am.

This temple resembles ours in Hyte, which also has four stories, each story smaller and shorter than the one below. An outside staircase zigzags from level to level. The sanctuary is a square on the roof. A copper man as tall as the length of my arm steps out of the sanctuary door. He takes a pose on the threshold, his left leg lifted, his left arm raised.

The pose may be meant to threaten or inspire awe, but I swallow a laugh. He wears a short skirt. A length of cloth is draped across one shoulder. Taking slow steps, he descends the stairs.

Maybe his pace is slow because the hinges at his knees are poorly made. He creaks.

At last he steps down from the final stair. For politeness I sit to face him at eye level — but he begins to grow, and the temple behind him grows too.

I stand and scramble back.

My warki cries, "Zaqwerfybn!"

When it reaches its full size, the temple is as vast as the one in Hyte, and the copper man is at least eight feet tall. His hinges disappear. He looms over me.

The warki is babbling in a singsong rhythm. I turn to see it bob up and down in time with its jabber. The copper man leans down and thrusts his face close to mine.

His eyebrows are low. His eyes, which seem to stare at my chin, are rubies set in white marble. His mustache gives his mouth a downward curve. His curled beard hangs down his chest.

I look for a shred of kindness in his face and find none.

His voice rings out, like cymbals. "Greetings! Welcome to Wadir."

He's uttered words! Not gibberish.

"Th-thank you, Master."

"I am delighted to see you." He speaks without showing his teeth. "I am glad my high priestess brought you."

Oh. My warki is female. And the high priestess. Is he the high priest or more than a priest?

"M-may I ask two questions?"

He smiles a close-lipped smile. I wonder if he has teeth or a tongue or anything else. He may be copper skin over air.

"You may ask."

"What day is today?"

"It is the ninetieth day of the twenty-fifth month, a Lurday."

I've never heard of Lurday. And months have only thirty days, and there are only twelve of them.

How long until my sacrifice?

"Master, have you heard of a god named Admat?"

"I am called by many names. Admat may be one of them."

I throw myself on the ground but keep my head above the feathers. He is nothing like the Admat I've imagined. "As you wish, so it will be."

"As I wish."

The holy text says:

Faith needs no sign.
Let not the creation
Test the creator.

But I must find out if this is Admat. I'm so afraid, only breath comes out at first. Feathers flutter upward, and I have the additional fear that I'll sneeze. I force the words out, "F-forgive me. Are you invisible in the upper world?"

"Certainly."

He doesn't seem to mind my test. "Thank you. Are you visible only here? Only to warkis and to living visitors like me?"

He roars, "My warkis live!"

The warki prostrates herself at my side. "Rgnjioplder."

"My high priestess is not dead! I am not the god of the dead."

Silence. I wait, then venture to raise my head. "Your worshipers" — I spit out feathers — "are blessed. Does your rule extend to Hyte?"

He shouts, "My rule has the height of the rock sky. I command all things beneath it."

He's not Admat. "You are mighty."

If these warkis aren't the dead, then where do the dead go? To the west, as I was taught?

Admat may still be here, somewhere else. And I may be years searching for him. I should pluck a feather and leave.

"Arise."

The warki jumps up. I stand too. I wonder if the copper god might have water that's safe to drink and food that isn't mud.

His voice is pleasant again. "My worshipers come seeking the dead."

Is that why their eyes are sad?

He goes on. "I persuade them to stay. Then they keep one another here, for company."

Puru said the warkis would try to hold me.

"And why not remain? My worshipers live

186

eternally, an easy life, joyous and without care."

Ouch! Something has pricked my arm. I look down. Aaah! A feather has sprouted! My stomach turns. I yank out the feather. Another pushes through the same pore. A gray warki feather. I would throw up if any food were in me.

Maybe Puru was wrong. He may not know. He said he's never been here. Maybe one feather isn't enough. Quickly I pluck a feather from my warki's arm.

"Wsdrghuk!"

I hold out the feather and nothing happens. Perhaps I have to use it somehow.

The copper god thunders, "What is your name?"

I can experiment later. I thread the feather through the weave of my tunic an inch below the neckline.

"What is your name?"

"Kezi."

"Look at me!"

Startled, I do.

"Your name is not Kezi." The ruby eyes bore into me.

His eyes are flames. Oh! My head hurts. The flames! I can't close my eyes. I see Olus, ablaze. My parents, ablaze. Aunt Fedo, ablaze. Hyte, ablaze. Consumed.

187

I see black smoke that pales to white.

The smoke clears. A huge golden man, a god, stands before me. "Your name is Eshar." His voice is kind. "Welcome, Eshar, my new warki."

I am Eshar.

"Riffguhjip."

I turn.

A feathered creature offers me a goblet.

I'm so thirsty. I take the goblet, sniff, look inside. The liquid is violet, odorless. "Thank you." I fill my mouth.

For an instant the drink is unbearably sour. As I start to spit it out, it turns sweet and fruity. I down the entire draft.

The world spins. I stagger and almost fall.

The ground is no longer thick with feathers. It's now a grassy meadow dotted by tulips. Everything is bright. The lava bubbles are as brilliant as tiny suns.

The woman with me has friendly brown eyes. I don't know why I thought she was feathered when in fact she's wearing a wool cloak. An extraordinary cloak, like a rug with the yarn left long. I reach out to study the workmanship.

She lets me finger it. Soft. Warm.

"Are you hungry, Eshar?"

"Yes."

"Come then."

I can't simply leave the god who named me. "All praise . . ."

His back is to me as he mounts the steps that lead to his golden sanctuary. But wasn't the temple copper a moment ago? Wasn't the god copper?

I shrug. The god and the temple are gold now.

"Come!"

I follow the woman through a forest of pistachio trees. The unripe nuts are a cool green.

The woman says, "I am Taram, high priestess of Wadir. Eshar is such a pretty name!"

I rub my arms for warmth and wish I had a cloak like Taram's. My tunic is much too flimsy for the chilly air. A band of wool circles my right arm above the elbow. It's the one part of me that feels warm and looks proper.

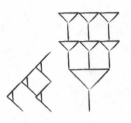

47

OLUS

Kezi has been in Wadir for three days. My annual festival is tomorrow, but I think only of her. What torments me most is that I might have saved her before she became endangered. After the oath, as soon as Fedo went in, I could have ridden my swift wind to Senat's house. I imagine the scene repeatedly: I barge into the house on some excuse, something about my goats. I say I've heard of Merem's illness and recovery. When Aunt Fedo tries to speak, I congratulate Senat and then the whole family.

Later Kezi marries someone — not Elon; a better man. She has the ordinary life she wants.

Night and day I'm plagued by images of her among the warkis. They mock her. She chases them to capture a feather. They back away, just out of reach. She wants me and wonders why I don't come.

I don't eat or sleep, but I pray to Admat. If there is an Admat, he may be the only one who can save her. If he's everywhere, he's with her in Wadir.

Soon after dawn on the morning of my festival, Hannu comes to my bedroom on the temple roof.

I'm in bed. "Every day I think Kezi will come today, and every night I think she will come tomorrow."

Holding my hand as if I were a child again, Hannu takes me to her room, where she and Ing, the goddess of love and beauty, help me bathe and dress.

"Smile during your festival," Hannu tells me, "or you'll terrify the soap bubbles."

My temple is in a field not far from Kudiya's hamlet. Kezi wouldn't think it a temple at all. The roof is flat, supported by columns rather than walls.

A wooden chair has been placed on the porch. Next to the chair, a small table holds a pitcher of therka and a goblet. I sit, but as soon as I do, I want to rise and pace. What will everyone think if I shout prayers to Admat?

An endless line of worshipers waits to my right at the edge of the porch. When I nod, the first one mounts the steps. How frightened he looks!

The man lays his gift at my feet, a basket filled with eggs. He asks for rain and tells me where he lives. I send rain clouds over his farm. He leaves. More worshipers file by with gifts. Many pray for favors I can't provide: a cow, gracefulness, a talent for playing the lyre. I promise to pass these prayers along to the respective gods.

Those prayers I can answer, I do. I clear clouds away or bring clouds. I warm the air or chill it. I prevent tunics from blowing off a clothesline, as one supplicant requests.

Some prayers are beyond the power of any Akkan god: for long life, happiness, the ability to fly. One old man asks me for optimism. His wife asks me for peace in her heart. I can no more give her peace or him optimism than they can give me Kezi. I recite a blessing.

Shortly after noon I see Kudiya in the line, the real Kudiya, with a sack hung over his shoulder. I wave him forward. Nonsensically I feel in his debt for my becoming a champion. When he reaches me, I grasp his arms and don't let him kneel.

"Kudiya! I am high and mighty to everyone, but not to one who's seen me pee."

His Adam's apple bobs in fear. He reaches

into his sack for his offering, a fig sapling, its roots wrapped in burlap, its branches sagging with ripe fruit, not a single unripe fig. I'm sure it's a portent. If I take it, Kezi will die. I signal a servant to take the tree.

Kudiya steps back, stammering apologies. Nervous whispers spread among the other worshipers.

When the tree has been removed, I struggle to collect myself. Finally I say, "What do you pray for?"

"N-never mind."

"Tell me."

Kudiya pulls from his sack a clay tablet covered with wedge writing.

The fig tree has unnerved me. I suspect Kudiya of being magical again — if not a vision this time, then a messenger bearing dire words about Kezi. With trepidation, I read:

Olus, god of the winds, who is your equal in mercy? This mortal begs your forbearance. Hannu, goddess of the earth, who gave pottery to humans, rages against her worshipers. Recently her earthquake destroyed half our village. Olus, mighty among the gods, this worshiper begs you to save us from her enmity.

I'm relieved enough to smile. "She isn't angry at you. When she isn't satisfied with her pots, she rampages." And the soap bubbles suffer.

Kudiya backs away, bowing.

"Wait! I can do something." I send my buffering wind to surround Hannu's workshop. With my wind at work, earthquakes will be reduced to tremors, landslides to a few rolling pebbles.

"Thank you, Olus, ruler of the winds."

On impulse I say, "Kudiya, would you stand at my side today?"

He pales but looks into my eyes for the first time. "Olus, what's wrong?"

"I'm alone. Please be at my side." He approaches, and we stand for hours, side by side. I'm soothed by his human presence. At sunset, when the last worshiper leaves, I thank him. "I need the friendship of mortals."

"Olus . . ." His Adam's apple bobs again, but he dares to clasp my shoulders. "I am your friend."

"I am your friend," I answer, and we part.

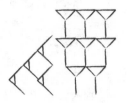

48
KEZI

My body is now covered in deliciously warm, many-colored threads of yarn. In appearance I am truly a warki. In spirit, maybe not. The other warkis are always smiling, and I am neither happy nor sad. A dozen sleepy mice seem to have made their home in my mind. When I try to think, a mouse curls up on the thought and snores. The thought collapses with a gentle *shoosh.*

Taram stays constantly at my side. I eat with her and the others, but without their delight, although everything tastes excellent. I rarely join in the conversation, which is always about whatever is occurring at the moment. I smile when everyone else laughs.

None of them mention the past, their own or mine.

After meals sometimes, Taram leads us to the temple of the golden god. We circle the temple once and bob up and down before it. The golden god never appears. When our worship is over, we march back through the pistachio forest to return to our ordinary activities.

I have two pleasures: weaving and watching the dancers. When I first arrived, I tried to join the dance but couldn't catch the rhythm. So I retreated to the loom. I don't know how my fingers learned their skill, but I am glad for it. The basket at my side holds wool in every tone I see in my coat, a vast selection. My fingers fly, and I have almost finished knotting a rug of Sinad, the stew warki, stirring his cauldron.

Taram praises my every choice of color and every new image. She is thrilled when I knot in Sinad's face. "The likeness is perfect!"

The mice in my mind wriggle happily.

Finally I am ready to knot in the upper border, where my name will go. I reach into the wool basket. *Eshar.* I don't know how to write my name.

I begin to feel distress, but the mice yawn.

Taram says, "It's time to worship. Come, Eshar!" She calls to the dancers and to the kitchen warkis. "Come!"

I leave my loom and follow her, surprised at the suddenness but relieved to delay the problem of knotting in my name. The other warkis crowd behind us.

On this occasion, she leads us three times around the temple rather than our usual single circuit. When we return to the front of the building, she prays aloud, which she has never done before. She thanks the golden god for our skills and compliments the dancers on their dance, the cooking warkis on their food, the potter on his pots, and so on, including a tribute to me for my rug. She ends by praising the golden god for giving us our beautiful world. I feel vague gratitude to him.

When she finishes, we return through the forest, and I find my loom empty. My rug has been taken off and stolen.

Outrage awakens in me. The mice grow less sleepy. The rug was mine, and I didn't even have a chance to put my name on it. I wonder if it was taken to stop me from weaving my name so someone else could claim it.

Taram says she doesn't know who stayed behind when we went to the temple. I don't know either. She says she's angry over the disappearance of my rug, but I'm suspicious of her for calling us to worship so abruptly.

I wind new warp on my loom. Not so much warp this time, for a narrow rug. I will knot in my name first — if I can.

"Will you depict Sinad again?" Taram asks.

I don't want her watching me weave. "No. A portrait of you, praying, as you did before the temple. But I need you to pose."

"A portrait of ugly me? No one will look at it."

"Everyone will look. You're high priestess."

She remains by my side while I begin to knot in a border.

"Don't you want to draw me first?" She saw me sketch Sinad in the dirt next to my loom before I began to knot him in.

I lie grandly. "You have inspired me. I will weave from life." As she watches, I create a thin border of yellow-and-purple triangles. The work goes quickly because the rug is so narrow. When the border is finished, I rise from my stool.

Feeling uneasy, I grasp her shoulders and move her far enough from the loom that she won't be able to see my knots. "Place your feet apart. You can relax your arms for now."

I return to my seat and look down at my loom. *Eshar.* I don't know how to write it. But when I think, I don't know how to knot rugs either. The knowledge is in my fingers. My fingers will make my name.

"How long will I have to stand here?"

"You can rest soon. Don't move your foot." I stare at Taram and don't look down. My fingers pull yarn out of my basket. I don't choose the colors. My heart races. I am not knotting *Eshar.*

"My feet hurt. I want to see."

"Stay another minute." I have only begun, but my name is coming to me.

"Eshar, I —"

Not *Eshar. Kezi!*

Taram is at my side. "Eshar, you didn't even start my feet!"

Kezi. My true name.

The mice flee. Memory returns. I am Kezi of Hyte, a dancer and a weaver.

Senat is my pado. Merem is my mati. Aunt Fedo is my aunt. Olus is my beloved. They are all far above and far away.

I smell mold again and sense the sadness in the air. When I look down at myself, I see with double vision, both the wool coat and the gray feathers. I am a horror, a creature, a warki. My arms and legs are feathered. My tunic bulges over feathers. Only the palms of my hands, my fingertips, and the bottoms of my feet are bare. I touch the soft down on my face. Oh! Ugh! I swallow repeatedly to keep from gagging.

How much time has passed? Are the figs

all ripe? Is my month over? Do my parents think I've abandoned them to Admat's fury?

Olus must miss me. I miss him. Puru said I'll be here forever. I'll never see Olus again.

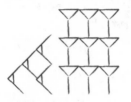

49
OLUS

When Kezi has been in Wadir for eight days, Puru appears before me on the temple roof.

I rush away from him, shouting to Admat, "Save Kezi. As you wish, so it will be." My festival was four days ago, and now I am wild again, filthy, unshaven, starving. But I'm sane enough to want to drown out whatever Puru has come to say. "Admat! Mighty one! Save Kezi. As you wish, so it will be."

Puru waits. An hour passes before I will listen. Finally I quiet.

"I . . . fear . . . it . . . is too late for your Kezi. She must have sprouted feathers by now. She will not return."

I call my swift wind and my wailing wind.

"She . . . has . . . reached . . . her destiny."

My winds and I shriek high across the mountains of Akka, the hills of Hyte, the other city-kingdoms of the south. Mortals run into their houses. Sheep race in circles. Birds dive out of the air.

I am the god of loneliness and grief.

A day and night of this and I circle back to Enshi Rock at dawn. Even if Kezi must remain in Wadir, we needn't be apart. I'll join her and grow feathers too. We'll make a nest and roost together, dead immortals in the netherworld.

I go to Puru's hut. He stands between his bed and his painted chest, juggling nine silver sticks, miraculously keeping them in the air despite his wrapped fingers. I tell him my plan.

"Endure . . . what . . . you . . . must endure."

Death. "When I'm safely dead, tell Hannu and Arduk."

He nods while juggling. "Your . . . winds . . ."

Without my control, they'll rage. "I'll contain all but my gentlest winds."

I take a huge jug from the temple kitchen, one of Hannu's by its shape. Then I fly off Enshi Rock on my smooth wind. I savor gliding on this, my last flight but one.

It's time for me to sacrifice myself. Admat, is this what you want? My death? The death of a god? All along, have you schemed for this?

On the lip of the volcano I put down my jug and begin to draw my winds into it. They curl in slowly, reluctantly. I coax in the ones I want to imprison and keep out the ones that can safely roam free.

50
KEZI

Taram approaches me, carrying a goblet.

I hear, both at once, "Pfhisxtrooou," and "Aren't you thirsty?"

Although I drank a few minutes before, I am very thirsty, but I shake my head.

I close my left eye. Wadir is bright and gay. I open my left eye and close my right. Wadir is dim and dreary.

I place my hand over my left ear.

"Are you hungry? I can . . ."

I'm starving. I move my hand to cover my right ear.

"Nflusqrthbla."

"Taram . . ." I say, still blocking sound in my right ear. I don't hear myself say *Taram*. Instead I hear *Jbomnc*. Again, I say, "Taram," and now I hear *Rzsoipkb*.

I think that warkis speak dream talk in which words change.

"Yes, Eshar?" Taram says. "Udmnhpl."

The name *Eshar* almost robs me of my memory again. *Kezi.* I pluck a feather from my thigh. It comes out easily, although the plucking hurts. The tip of a new feather instantly pokes through the pore.

I remember Puru's last words. *Fate may be thwarted. I long for a happy outcome.*

"Taram? Is there a way out of Wadir?"

"Where else is there, Eshar?"

Kezi! It was the wrong question. I try again. "Where did you come from?"

"I began here, silly Eshar."

The repetition of *Eshar* is having an effect. "I'm silly Kezi."

"And you're thirsty, silly Eshar." Taram holds out the drink.

The mice invade my mind again. I accept the goblet and raise it to my lips. But the foul smell wakes me. Kezi.

I wonder if Taram had another name once, if she came seeking someone she loved and the golden god took her memories too. "What was your first name, Taram?"

Taram drops the goblet. Her down-lashed eyes weep. "I don't know." She starts away from me. After a few steps, she turns. "It was Taram! As yours is Eshar."

Kezi! I turn my back on her and march through the kitchen and past the dining warkis.

She calls after me, "Silly Eshar, you'll drink when you're thirsty enough."

Kezi! I won't. Better eternal thirst and hunger than no thoughts and no memory. The gloomy air asks, Truly better? Knowing you're forever separated from Olus? Knowing your mati and pado suffered when you didn't return to fulfill the oath?

I wave my hands around my head, fending off the air itself. The brook of violet liquid is a few yards ahead.

A hand grips my shoulder.

"Taram . . ." I say. But the hand is gold — copper — both. The warki god!

"Where are you going, Eshar?"

Kezi!

He turns me. I can't resist his strength, but I look down. I don't want to meet his eyes again!

"Eshar . . ." His hands tilt my head up.

I close my eyes and shout, "Kezi! Kezi! Kezi!"

One hand grips the back of my head. "Eshar." A finger lifts my left eyelid. The metal nail digs in below my eyebrow.

I focus downward. We are motionless. He doesn't let go. He cannot move my eyeball, but he can squeeze my head. My ear and scalp burn.

Finally he says, "I won't keep you against

your will." His finger leaves my eyelid. He lifts me by my head and shoulder and hurls me across the violet stream.

Aaa! I slam down. The breath shoots out of me. If it weren't for my own feathers and the feathers on the ground, my back would be broken.

I scramble up and limp off as quickly as I can, not looking to see if he is behind me. When my knees give out, I collapse.

If he'd pursued me, he'd have caught me. I dare to peek. He is gone. The warkis are small and dim in the distance. I sit up. Lightly, I touch my eyelid. My finger when I bring it away is not bloody. A relief, but my head and ear throb.

I haven't escaped. The stairs to the upper world disappeared when I arrived here — and I couldn't climb them anyway.

I yank feathers out of my arms and legs. New feathers grow in as quickly as the old come out. Both the plucking and the new growth burn. Imps of pain race along my skin.

After a few minutes I give up the plucking. I'm still a warki. At least I can continue my search for Admat.

But I want Olus more than I want him. Forgive me, Admat! Olus is more real to me than you are.

I watch the lava bubbles drift overhead toward the other warkis. If I walk against the tide of bubbles, I should reach the bottom of the volcano. Maybe from there I can see the sky.

I stand and set out, no longer needing to limp. Gradually the carpet of feathers thins, exposing bare patches of packed dirt. The lava bubbles crowd together overhead. Before me is a thick mist. I hear hissing and gurgling. Thank you, Admat! Thank you, any gods who may be watching over me.

I run into the mist. Soon I am standing under a rock arch at the edge of the lava lake, which seethes and steams. I can't see the sky through the fog, but I know that above is the world of mortals and gods and night and day.

What day?

The air is fresher here. Rock walls rise on either side of me. They must be the bowl of the volcano.

Can a warki climb out?

On my right the rock is smooth, but on my left a ledge curves upward. The ledge is above my head, and few handholds or footholds lead up to it. If I fall, I'll boil in lava.

I take off my sandals and slip them onto my arms, like bracelets. I need bare feet to have a chance at reaching the ledge. It is lucky that my fingertips and the bottoms of my feet are free of feathers.

The mud at the edge of the lava lake simmers. Hopping in place, I find fingerholds in the rock.

Admat! Olus! Puru! Any god who can help me! Make me able to lift my legs and climb. Mati! Pado! Aunt Fedo! Pray for me! Let me climb!

I can! I position my hands and feet carefully and climb, clinging to whatever I can find: chinks, cracks, tiny nicks. I am panting from fear and strain. After I catch my breath, I climb again. When I've placed myself a third time, the ledge is within reach. Muscles straining, I hoist myself up. Sitting tight against the wall, I don my sandals and stand.

The ledge is littered with rocks, and a few yards ahead it disappears into the lava mist. Still, it leads upward. I hurry. My month may not be over.

I halt, remembering. Olus may have failed at his championship trial. He may be trapped somewhere.

Maybe I can help him.

A hundred years may have passed. He may have forgotten me. My family may have died long ago.

The ledge slants steeply upward. I climb. The chill air of Wadir warms. I strain for speed. My breath comes in gasps, but I fight onward. Finally I have to rest. I turn to see how far I've come. The mist obscures the view, but what I do see is a trail of feathers. I'm shedding!

A few feathers poke from the pores on my arms. When I brush at them, they fall off and are not replaced. They drop off my legs too. I hold the tunic away from my body, and a shower of feathers falls on the path. Hardly daring to hope, I touch my face.

The down is gone! I am no longer a warki. And, without my noticing, I am no longer racked with hunger and thirst.

The only feather I still have is Taram's, threaded below the neckline of my tunic. I'll save it to show Puru when I tell him how I thwarted fate — if an end in Wadir was my fate. Maybe I was always destined to find my way out.

I laugh. Maybe it is all foolishness: fate, Puru's advice, Admat, the claims of the warki god.

I continue up the path as the mist begins to clear.

51
OLUS

It is noon before my wildest winds are caught in the jug. My tame winds I leave free, including my herding wind, which is still guarding my goats. My buffering wind continues to cushion Hannu's workshop. I hope they will keep at their tasks, but if not, so be it.

In my mind I apologize to Hannu and to Arduk for not saying farewell. I couldn't risk them stopping me.

Kezi, I am on my way to you.

I leap off the edge of the volcano.

52
KEZI

The mist is below me. I look up for my first sight of the sky.

A new warki?

Its arms and legs are splayed, its face rapt. Olus! He came for me!

But he's falling, not riding a wind. Thoughts come in a rush. I can't save him. I can die with him. Fate may be thwarted.

No happy outcome, unless —

As Olus falls, I pull Taram's feather from my tunic. The instant I touch it, the feather multiplies. Wings form. Muscle and sinew and bone grow on them. A body takes shape: head, neck, torso, legs, hooves, mane, tail. In a blink the feather becomes a winged stallion, wheeling and banking and fairly begging me to leap onto his back.

I do leap and hug his sides with my legs. The horse dives and sweeps Olus up as he enters the lava steam, settling him behind me, on his belly, hanging across the animal's wide back. I reach back to take his hand.

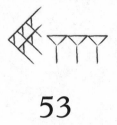

53
OLUS

I raise my head. Kezi?

It happens so quickly. I die and become a warki in a second. Wadir must have winged steeds just as Enshi Rock does, although this one is gray and ours are white. I roll over, straddle the horse, and circle Kezi's waist with my arms. I lean into her shoulders and breathe her in. Cinnamon, yes, but also mold and sadness. Is she sad to be dead? Is she sad I've come?

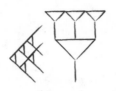

54

KEZI

We pass over the lip of the volcano. I grasp the stallion's mane and guide him down the mountain, although he seems to need no guidance.

Olus was willing to die for me. He would become mortal, Puru said, if he followed me to Wadir.

The wind is bracing. I let go of the horse's mane to raise my arms and wriggle my fingers. I smell pine, not mold. The trees are alive. Every breath makes me want to smile, not weep. The sky is cloudy. Enshi Rock is hidden.

I wish Senat and Merem and Aunt Fedo could see me on this flying steed.

The stallion flies over a river, then a strip of trees, and lands in a meadow. Olus and I dismount, and the huge creature begins to graze.

Olus kisses me. He's growing a beard. The hairs tickle.

After the kiss, he murmurs into my hair, "Where are our feathers?" He sounds disappointed.

For a moment I don't understand. Then I'm laughing against his shoulder.

He holds me out at arm's length, his expression puzzled.

Oh dear, he thinks he's dead and wants his feathers. It takes me a few minutes to get out, "We're not warkis. This is Mount Enshi."

His face is so surprised, I laugh even harder.

He begins to laugh too.

Real laughter is the opposite of Wadir. Gradually we sober.

"You saved my life."

"You were going to die for me."

"I was going to find you."

A bird trills. I've never heard anything sweeter.

"You're a heroine now. You escaped from Wadir."

I take this in. A heroine. The first step to becoming immortal. I sit and watch an ant crawl through the grass.

"I couldn't count the days down there." I'm afraid to look up. "Has the day of my sacrifice passed?"

"Not yet."

"When?"

"Fifteen days after today."

Nine days lost in Wadir. Only nine days. He might have said nine years and I wouldn't have been surprised. I'm grateful, and yet . . . Nine days out of the twenty-five I had when I entered the tunnel. Nine days of sky and sun and kisses.

Olus sits next to me.

I lean against his shoulder. "If you had fallen into the lava, I don't think you would have become a warki."

"No? I was mortal as soon as I jumped." He folds his fingers over mine.

"The warkis are not the dead." I tell him about Wadir.

He listens. Sometimes he says "Oh, Kezi" in such a soft, sorrowful, and respectful way.

The respect is the most soothing of all. My tears spill out. "The warki god said his worshipers are not the dead, but they come seeking the dead."

"Did you see new ones come?"

I shake my head. "To go into the moldy earth . . . few would do it. People must be grieving terribly. They probably cause the melancholy in the air. Taram wept when I asked her what her name used to be. Her eyes were always sad. I'm glad I won't go there if I die. I'm glad Pado and Mati and Aunt Fedo won't."

He kisses me.

I could let him comfort me, but I need to confess. I pull away. "I didn't find Admat. A believer would have looked longer. No, a believer wouldn't have had to look at all. I don't know what happens when anyone dies. We could each have a different afterlife or no afterlife at all."

He strokes my cheek with the backs of his fingers. "We can go to Enshi Rock. You can come now, and I can take you."

"Yes? You're a champion!"

He nods, smiling.

"Were you shut in somewhere?"

"You guessed! You were thinking of me?"

"Yes, I was thinking about you!"

He tells me about the well and the spiders and the bees. "I am no longer afraid. If you'd like, we could live in the cave behind the falls of Zago."

I smile, but I'm thinking how awful it must have been for him. "Why couldn't they have just let you bring me to Enshi Rock?" I realize I'm criticizing the Akkan gods, but I don't stop. "Why did we have to be tested?"

Olus's smile becomes a frown. "I don't

218

know." After a moment, he adds, "Why do you have to be sacrificed?"

"The oath laws. Oh!" If there is no Admat . . . "Who made the oath laws?"

"I don't know."

A different god? People?

55
OLUS

While Kezi walks to the river to scrub off the stench of Wadir, I ride her winged steed to the jug at the edge of the volcano.

My winds exit in a trice. I dispatch my clever wind and my fetching wind on an errand. Then I ride the stallion to a higher bend in the river, where I bathe too and shave off my beard.

Soon Kezi will try to become immortal. If she fails, we'll have two weeks. Now that I know the truth about Wadir, I won't have even the consolation of following her there.

After my bath, I return to the meadow, where my fetching wind has already left a big sack. While the stallion grazes, my clever wind opens the sack, sets up the table and chairs. I command my hot wind to keep the warm food warm and my chill wind to keep the cold food cold. I command my barrier wind to prevent the scents from straying to

Kezi and spoiling the surprise. My clever wind arranges plates, bowls, and tumblers, all of them Hannu's creations.

The horse would like to share our meal, but my barrier wind keeps him away.

Everything is ready. Ready. Ready.

How long can she take to bathe?

Perhaps a current has caught her. Or a snake has bitten her. I listen for distant noises and hear her singing and splashing.

"Left foot, right foot.
Heel, toe.
Dunk face . . ."

Now gurgling laughter.

I wait and wait. At last I hear her surge out of the water. A few minutes later she calls, "I had no soap, but I scrubbed and —" She emerges at the edge of the trees and stops, looking astonished. I grin like a fool and let my barrier wind release the scents.

"From Enshi Rock?"

"From the kitchen of the Akkan gods." Only therka is missing. I pull a chair out for her.

Instead of sitting, she examines the chair, which is made of golden oak. On each side is a low relief of people walking, arms raised, holding up the armrest. She runs her fingers along the carving. The seat is leather. She leans her palm into it, then finally sits.

I take the other chair.

She tilts her plate up. The rim is tan and turquoise, the colors bleeding into each other and rising in peaks toward the center. Behind the peaks a gray sky swirls.

"My mati Hannu made the plates."

"There's a countryside in this one. If we were tiny, we could go into it. Your winds could carry us to a peak. What would we see far away?"

I grin. "An enormous bowl of goat stew."

"Huge mutton chops."

"Would you like an actual duck egg?" I give her a boiled egg from a pile of a dozen and take one too. Then I pour pomegranate juice into each of our tumblers.

She touches the egg. "It's still warm, and the shell isn't cracked."

"My clever wind is very clever." I feel ridiculously proud. "The bean patties are excellent."

She nods and takes one. "Mmm." Her face changes. She puts the patty down. "Olus?"

"Yes?"

She leans back in her chair. "I'm being silly, but . . ."

"Please tell me."

"The food. In Wadir it was mud. When I was Eshar, the mud tasted and looked and smelled like duck eggs or stew or soup. What if this delicious food is really . . ." She shrugs. I see she's on the verge of tears.

I rub her back, wishing I knew the right words to say. I remember the bees and the spiders and Kudiya who wasn't Kudiya. This food *could* be mud.

"What if *Kezi* isn't my true name? And not *Eshar* either." She takes my hand, turns up the palm, and traces the lines in it. "What if I were told my truest name and then I would be someone else and have a pado who never swore an oath and there would be no need for me to be sacrificed or to try to be immortal?"

Then I might still be Olus, but there would be no Kezi. I clasp her hand, and she squeezes mine.

"It may all be a dream," I say. "No matter what anyone wishes, so it would be."

"So it would be." She nods. "Who knows what my truest name would make me? So it would be." After a moment she smiles and picks up her bean patty.

I don't like that smile, so sad it's barely a smile at all.

"What else do the Akkan gods dine on?"

she asks.

"Therka is our drink, but I couldn't bring any." I load her plate with catfish, beets, barley, and turnips. As I dish out the turnips, I say, "My pado, Arduk, calls me Turnip. It's his name for me."

The smile loses its sadness. "Turnip?"

"Turnip."

She shakes her head wonderingly. "My love is a god called Turnip." She giggles.

"He may name you Garlic."

"I like garlic."

Dusk falls. We end our meal with dates and pistachios. My clever wind brought no figs.

"Thank you for this meal." Kezi licks her fingers. "Olus? Does the test for immortality take long?"

"Only a moment."

"A moment to decide everything?"

"Yes."

"So I could wait almost until the end, right?"

I nod. In case she can't see me in the deepening twilight, I say, "Yes."

"I have fourteen days after today. You can show me Akka before we have to know the future. Let's not hurry."

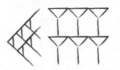

56
KEZI

We bed down in the meadow. Olus wraps us in his warm wind, which is both mattress and blanket. He kisses me good night and then kisses me again more lingeringly. I slide closer. My hand strokes his arm, his back.

"Kezi . . ." He draws away.

"If I die . . ." I whisper, moving near again.

"Shh."

In the morning we breakfast on yesterday's leavings, almost as much a feast as it was last night. I pile the dishes until he tells me to stop. His winds will return everything to Enshi Rock. We can leave.

I dance to my horse, who raises his head, his lips trailing grass. He needs a name. I rub his muzzle until his name comes to me. "Your name is Kastu." *Kastu* means *silver.* Grasping his mane, I throw myself on his back. "Let's race!"

Kastu's wings beat the air. We rise.

225

I turn, looking for Olus.

He's behind and falling farther behind, stroking the air desperately, his face red. I pull back on Kastu's mane and see Olus's grin begin. The god called Turnip is a clown! I lower my head to Kastu's neck and urge him to his greatest speed.

He stretches himself. The wind whips my hair back and stings my ears. Olus catches up easily and circles us, lying on his back, arms folded, feet crossed at the ankles, completely at ease.

I have never laughed so hard.

A moment later he comes to ride behind me on Kastu's back, so we can talk and be close.

We circle Mount Enshi and head for Neme, the only city in Akka. It is much smaller than Hyte. The houses are made of wood, and the streets are paved with stones. Olus takes me to the temple, a semicircular wall of marble blocks, sacred to Ursag, the god of wisdom. Words have been chiseled into the wall.

This is a temple? A wall covered with writing in a script I don't recognize? "What do the words mean?"

"They're a selection of Ursag's writings." Olus reads: " 'Lend to strangers; give to friends.' 'A man of bad character can never acquire knowledge.' 'It is —' "

"A woman of bad character can?"

He smiles. "Tell Ursag. He loves to debate."

I don't know if I'll be able to argue with the god of wisdom, but I think that a smart man or woman can easily acquire knowledge.

Olus reads on. " 'Widows and orphans owe no taxes.' "

"We have the same law!"

" 'No plea to a judge has been made unless it has been made in writing.' "

I'd better learn to read and write if . . .

"There are hundreds of adages here, thousands in the library on Enshi Rock."

What would be the right dance for the god of wisdom? Something measured. I dip my head. My arms describe slow circles in the air. I turn, then twist from the waist. There are many twists and turns in the thoughts of the wise.

Olus is smiling with such pleasure that I almost stumble. When I finish dancing, we leave Neme behind and fly over forests and meadows and streams before the sun sets. Everywhere, I compare Akka with Hyte. Hyte has wider roads and flatter land for planting. But Akka has rushing rivers, and the mountains are grand.

Over the next twelve days Olus takes me to every fine viewpoint he knows. I watch as his winds make cloud shadows slide across the hills. We visit the ruins of ancient Akkan temples to unknown gods. We pass two days at the falls of Zago, talking, talking, talking — about what we think, what we feel, what's happened to us. But never about what will happen.

The twelfth day we spend riding a single-masted boat down one of Akka's rivers. The banks glide by, while I clasp Olus's hand and try to hold back the minutes. I want the river to stop flowing. The sail can continue to billow, but we must not move. Olus's winds must blow time itself away and stretch this moment into eternity.

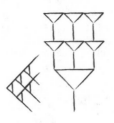

57
OLUS

The air is cold with the promise of autumn when I awaken at dawn on our last day but one. We are back at the falls of Zago. Kezi is several feet from me, still asleep in her wind cocoon, lying on her side, her hand cradling her cheek.

I imagine her lying this way on the temple altar in Hyte, lulled to sleep by prayer chants.

Stop! She will become immortal.

Before anything else, we will need breakfast, and the Zago teems with trout. I make a fire. In a few minutes a big fish wriggles in my arms. I drop it on the riverbank and take out my knife. While the fish flops and flails, I stand over it. My appetite vanishes, and my arm trembles until I drop the knife.

Kastu whinnies.

Kezi leans on her elbow and watches me throw the fish back into the river.

"I didn't like the looks of it," I say. "We can breakfast on the remains of dinner." I douse the fire.

My fetching wind brings a loaded platter out from the cave behind the falls, where we stored yesterday's food. It sets the platter down between the two stone chairs.

"Olus, how many gods and goddesses are there?"

"You will be the forty-eighth." I recite, "Abdi, Adda, Addi, Aham, Ahum, Ahur . . . *A* is the most popular first letter."

"What is Abdi the god of?" She stretches.

"Cleanliness and laundry."

"A god for those! Is there a god for slipper- and sandal-making?" She sits up. "I'm glad you're not the god of chicken plucking!"

I'm a little offended. "There *is* Jawa, the goddess of fowl, who gave mortals chicken plucking. Doesn't Admat oversee these matters too?"

"I never thought about Admat and everyday things. Only Admat and war or drought or flood or illness." She smiles wistfully. "And Mati, Pado, Aunt Fedo, and me." She stands and tries to smooth out her wrinkled tunic. Looking down, she says, "Are all the goddesses beautiful?"

"Not Cala."

"I forgot who she is."

"The goddess of wild and tame animals, who used to be mortal. Before she became a goddess, her cheek was raked by a lion. She has a scar."

Kezi squats and splashes river water on her face. "The rest are all beautiful," she says flatly.

"Ursag is almost as tall as a giraffe. I don't know how Puru looks."

"They're not goddesses." She straightens and combs her hair back with her fingers.

I've been saying the wrong things. "*You're* beautiful." I hug her and kiss her hair. And I send my clever wind to Enshi Rock.

"Thank you." She breaks away and goes to the platter. "What would you like?"

"I'm not hungry."

She nods. After loading her plate with everything we have left, she sits in one of the stone chairs and eats with obvious relish. I drop into the other chair and watch her — her hands, her face, the dancer's way she sits — gathered, as if she could spring into a graceful leap at any moment.

Finally the last morsel is gone. She says, "Don't look!"

I obey, although it doesn't matter if I look

or not. I know she's licking drops of honey off her plate.

"There. You can look." She puts her plate down on the grass at her feet and stands.

A parcel wrapped in burlap lands with a thump on the chair she just rose from.

"What's this?"

My nimble wind unwraps the burlap. I'm smiling.

"Oh!"

A tunic for her is on top, mine underneath. She runs her hand over hers, then unfolds it. "Is that gold thread?" She points to the embroidery at the hem.

I stand. "Probably." My clever wind is very clever.

She picks up the sash.

"Green for good fortune," I say.

She blushes. "Green for marriage." She lays her tunic down on the other stone chair and picks mine up. "It's the color of iron. The exact color. You have a dye this color on Enshi Rock?"

"We must. Ahum is the god of cloth and weaving." There is green in my tunic, too, along the hem.

She holds my tunic up against me. "Splendid."

While she's so close, I kiss her.

"Olus . . ." She turns and places the tunic

carefully atop the burlap. "If I die —"

"Shh!"

"Let me talk. If I die, keep looking for Admat."

"I will." If she dies, I'll have my revenge on Admat, if I find him, and I'll certainly take revenge on his priests.

"Comfort my parents and Aunt Fedo. Watch over them."

I choose my words so that I promise nothing. "You mustn't worry." I may not have the compassion to comfort her family. I may revenge myself on them, too.

"When I'm dead, I may not be able to think of you. There —"

"Stop!"

"If I die . . ." She touches my cheek. "If I die . . ."

I kiss her and taste the honey on her breath.

"I love you now," she says. "I love you immortally, even if I die and there is nothing left of me."

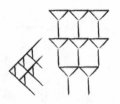

58
KEZI

I was so brave at breakfast! And now, flying on Kastu to Enshi Rock, I am terrified. I may vomit my courage down over Akka.

Admat, I pray, wherever you may be, if you may be, let me live. Let me pass the gods' test. I didn't want to be immortal before. I know I said so. But I want to live, so please forget my earlier wish and let me become immortal.

I rest my head on Kastu's neck. Kastu, give me horse valor. Let me do my best.

Olus is next to me on one of his winds. I looked at him once but not again. His face was stamped with worry.

We are high above Akka. This time clouds don't close in. Olus's winds do not fail him. Enshi Rock grows until it blocks out the sun and all but a trimming of sky. The rock's underside is forbidding, nothing but spikes and fangs of dirty yellow stone.

Two winged steeds push off the top edge and fly toward us. Sentries come to warn us away?

"Hannu!" Olus shouts. "Arduk!"

His parents! I lace my fingers in Kastu's mane.

They fly close. How can they be thousands of years old? They seem barely older than I am.

After circling once, they join us. Hannu flies on Olus's left, Arduk on my right. Arduk has silky black hair just as Olus does.

He smiles. "Green Bean," he says, "so you're the girl our Turnip admires."

Loves and admires.

Green Bean? He's nicknamed me! I blush and smile and can't think of anything to say. Finally: "Akka is beautiful."

"Hannu made the earth and I made the plants. Enshi Rock is beautiful too."

We are rising next to a cliff of the same ugly yellow stone as the rock's bottom. I dare to glance at Hannu, who has pulled Olus close to her and linked her arm in his.

He says, "This is Kezi, Hannu. Kezi, this is my mati. Hannu, be welcoming."

"What would I be?" She turns a brilliant smile on me and waves.

I bow my head. She could hate me behind

her smile. I'm certain only that she is the most magnificent woman I've ever seen. Olus has her wide mouth and brown eyes, but not her elegant eyebrows. Her legs gripping her mount are athletic and graceful. Her arms are as finely modeled as her pottery.

"Kezi!"

I turn to Olus.

"We've arrived."

We rise above Enshi Rock. I look down. The edge is a ribbon of grass. We fly over a narrow peninsula. I see rows of stone seats circling a tiled floor. Men and women fill the first few rows. A woman addresses them.

Not men and women. Gods and goddesses! My stomach tightens.

"Hannu made the peninsula to hold the amphitheater," Arduk says. "Enshi Rock widens ahead."

He is kind to be my guide, although I can hardly pay attention. Soon I'll know my fate. My ears drum *soon soon soon.*

"Below is my farm, Green Bean. There's my garden. I planted certain flowers for contrast and others to blend into each other."

Try to concentrate. I may never see this again.

Two gods sit on a bench. A goddess stands nearby.

Oh! There's a hole in the center of the garden!

No. Not a hole. A lake that perfectly reflects the blue sky. We cross it, and I see the bellies of the three steeds, their tucked-in legs, and the undersides of their enormous wings.

Ahead is an extraordinary tower, made of a single tall stone. It's a white finger poking from the center of Enshi Rock.

I turn to Olus. "What is that?"

Arduk answers. "Our temple, Green Bean. Our home. Hannu made it." I hear the pride in his voice.

As we approach, I see windows and, on the roof, a canopy. Olus's place, he's told me.

We land in a paddock near a stable. I rub Kastu's nose. Give me good fortune, Kastu.

"Kezi!" Hannu opens her arms. "You saved my son! I saw you rise from the volcano with him."

Olus touches my shoulder, I think to give me confidence, which certainly I need.

She pulls me into a hug. After a moment she holds me at arm's length. "He would have died for you. How I hated you! But you saved him." Her eyes search my face.

237

She is judging me.

I stop breathing and meet her eyes. Is this the test? Is Olus's mati my judge?

Whatever she sees, she says, "You are worthy of my son's love." She pulls me close again.

"Th-thank you," I mumble over her shoulder.

She releases me. "I hope you will be my daughter."

Hope. This was not the test.

Arduk says, "We both hope you will be our daughter, Green Bean." He crouches and cups his hand over a patch of grass.

"Arduk . . ." Olus says.

"Patience, Turnip," he murmurs. His eyes are closed.

The rest of us wait in silence, although I'm not sure why we're waiting.

Arduk opens his hand. Small flowers climb a tall stalk. Their orange petals are shot through with white veins. I could weave a rug of a single blossom, if I ever weave another rug.

Arduk stands. "In your honor."

I swallow. "Thank you."

Olus takes my hand. "Where is the ceremony?"

"In Ursag's library, Turnip."

"In the temple," Olus tells me.

We follow an avenue lined with date palms. I put one foot in front of the other and grip Olus's hand as tight as I can.

Compared to the temple I feel as tiny as a rabbit. The temple is raised on four legs, each about three times my height. Hannu leads us up the staircase that circles one leg. At the top we enter through a white-painted wooden door into an indoor staircase. We climb past a landing and a door, another landing, another door, another, and another. I remember the tunnel down to Wadir. Now I'm in a tunnel going up, just as frightened as I was then.

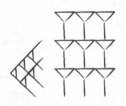

59
OLUS

This is fear. The bees and the spiders and Kudiya in the well were shivers compared to what I feel as we enter the temple library.

Ursag's voice calls, "Come!"

We file down the narrow center aisle between shelves that sag with the weight of the tablets they hold. Kezi precedes me and lets my hand go. I open and close my empty fingers. From behind me Hannu presses the flat of her hand between my shoulder blades.

Puru and Ursag are silhouetted against a bright window. Ursag leans over a table and pours therka into six goblets. Puru holds something in the folds of his linens.

Ever since Kezi left the Hyte market with me, we've been traveling toward this gathering.

"Puru!" Kezi runs toward him. She opens

her arms as though to embrace him, but stops short and only touches his shoulder. I've never seen anyone else touch him.

He doesn't move, except his chin comes up a little.

Puru, help her! I think. Nudge destiny!

"Thank you, Puru," she says. "Your words saved me."

"What . . . words . . . ?"

" 'Fate may be thwarted.' "

" 'I . . . long . . . for . . . a happy outcome.' "

"I sprouted feathers, but I left Wadir."

"Yes . . ."

I feel as if I'm miles away, watching everyone from the pasture with my goats.

Hannu bursts out of the aisle. "We hope she will be our daughter, Puru."

"Hope . . . and . . . fate . . . live in separate houses."

"This is no time for enigmas," I say, irritated. Help her!

"No . . ."

"Turnip, he means hope has no influence over fate."

Of course. But Kezi has suffered enough. I want to spill the therka out the window.

"Ursag," Arduk adds, "we've brought the heroine Kezi to you."

Ursag puts down the therka. Two goblets

241

have yet to be filled. "Kezi!" he says. "Welcome to Enshi Rock."

She turns from Puru. "Thank you." Her face is awed.

With his shaggy hair, Ursag is a date palm leaning over her. "Heroes and heroines are revered on Enshi Rock above gods and mortals alike."

She blushes. "Thank you."

"Champions, too, Turnip."

"Puru has a gift for each of you," Ursag adds.

Puru holds out two clay tablets. Balanced on each is a green limestone seal. I see Puru's fingers for the first time. The god of destiny bites his fingernails.

I reach for a tablet and seal.

"No . . ." Puru crosses his arms.

I take the correct ones but don't look at them. Instead I watch Kezi receiving hers. She puts the seal down on the table with the therka and the goblets and traces the figures on the upper half of the tablet, where her story is told in low relief.

"Olus, look! Here I am, coming down the stairs. This is the stream I crossed. That's a warki. Look! There you are, falling into the volcano, and there's Kastu. But the warki god isn't in it. You don't know about him, do you, Puru?"

"Warki . . . god . . . ?"

"He rules the warkis. Olus, what do the words say?"

" 'Kezi of Hyte, daughter of Senat and Merem, traveled to Wadir, overcame hunger and thirst, sprouted feathers, shed feathers as no one had done before, climbed out of Wadir as no one had done before, and saved the god of the winds to become a heroine of Akka. Much praise to heroine Kezi of Hyte.' "

"Oh!"

I believe I know what she's thinking: that she has the tablet and seal no matter what comes next. I disagree. She can't take the seal and the tablet to the grave.

"Let me see yours," she says.

I put my seal on the table next to hers and tilt the tablet toward her. It depicts a bee and a spider and me, all the same size, then another image of me, climbing a rock wall with Kudiya.

"Read it, please."

" 'Olus of Akka, god of the winds, son of Arduk and Hannu, endured bees and spiders, conquered his fear of confinement, succored Kudiya of Akka, carried him from a well during an earthquake as no god had done before, to become a champion of Akka. Much praise to champion Olus of

Akka.' "

Hannu picks up Kezi's seal. "I will make pots of your triumphs."

"Kezi can knot rugs," I say. If she lives.

Ursag fills the remaining goblets. I stop breathing. In a moment we'll know.

60
KEZI

Puru gives me a goblet. The beverage is
golden colored, too syrupy to be apple juice,
not syrupy enough to be honey. I wait for
someone else to drink. When will the test
come? The day is half over.

"What do you hope to be goddess of?"
Ursag says.

The test is coming soon or he wouldn't be
asking. I haven't thought of the kind of goddess I should be. I look at Olus.

He smiles at me, but it's not a real smile.
How frightened he is!

I can't be goddess of anything important.
How can I be? "Goddess of the dances of
Hyte?"

"Bunda is the goddess of dance, Green
Bean. She won't want to give up any
dances."

I remember that there is a god of weaving.
I turn the goblet in my hand.

Everyone waits. The linens over Puru's

fingers flutter. I think he may be frightened too.

What can I be goddess of? Admat, if he exists, is the god of everything. The Akkan gods probably need no one else. What's left?

It comes to me. "If I can, I will be the goddess of uncertainty."

Puru's shoulders slump. I've chosen wrong!

But Hannu cries, "Glorious!"

"Original," Ursag says. "We have no god or goddess of doubt."

They raise their goblets.

"This is therka, Kezi," Ursag says. "You will find it only on Enshi Rock."

"Drink, Green Bean."

"Wait!" In front of all of them, Olus kisses me on the lips.

The kiss alarms me more than anything. I'm embarrassed, too, but I understand it's the last kiss before my fate is decided, so I kiss him back.

Arduk coughs. Olus and I separate.

I taste the therka. The flavor is fruity and nutty. I roll it around in my mouth, savoring it. Then I try to swallow, but my throat closes. I try again, but I can't swallow. I see Olus's face. This is the test!

61
OLUS

Kezi's face turns red. Her eyes bulge.

I must do something! I thread my thinnest wind between her lips into her mouth to ease her throat open.

Her cheeks puff with my wind, but she seems unable to swallow. She spits the therka out. Therka runs down her chin.

She cannot become immortal.

62

Kezi

Ursag approaches, holding his hand out for my goblet.

"No!" I hold the goblet against my chest. "Puru, I long for a happy outcome."

"Kezi . . ."

"Yes?" Hannu says.

"It . . . is . . . over. . . ."

Ursag comes closer.

"No!" Olus cries.

I feel his wind whirl around me, keeping the others away. I put the goblet to my lips. Fate may be thwarted.

Again I take in therka and cannot swallow. As I hold it in my mouth, I imagine Admat's altar and the altar flame. In my mind I look directly into the flame.

With therka in my mouth and Olus's wind swirling, I bend my right knee and point my toes. I lean back on my left hip and glide into the next step.

As I dance I spit out the therka. But I

don't give up the goblet.

Hannu begins to clap. Arduk joins in. I have my beat. I thrust my right shoulder forward, then my left. Right hip forward, left. I raise my arms, still holding the goblet.

I chose the wrong kind of goddess to be. Puru's slumping shoulders told me so.

Sway. Turn.

People need an uncertainty deity. They should question the gods. The people of Hyte should doubt Admat's holy text and his wrath against his worshipers who love him.

Lower my arms. Don't spill the therka.

Hannu quickens the beat.

Dip. Step.

Hannu is the goddess of earth *and* pottery. Cala is the goddess of wild *and* tame animals. Abdi is the god of cleanliness *and* laundry. I can have more than one power.

Bend. Straighten.

Olus claps. Thank you, my love.

What else do mortals need that I can give them?

I remember Belet's wedding, the ecstasy of the dance, the sound of the copper rattle, the taste of the food. I remember Olus's lips in our first kiss.

Dip, step.

I remember Wadir, where the sleepy mice

dulled me, where I savored nothing and where I lost count of my days and nights.

Dip, slide.

Ursag claps. Puru taps his feet.

I know what else I can give.

63
OLUS

She stops dancing, but I continue to clap. "Dance, love!" I shout. "Don't give up!"

Looking at Puru, she raises the goblet and announces, "My power . . ."

I stop clapping.

". . . will be to save mortals from dreaming away their days. When people are forgetful, I'll bring them a color, a song, a scent, a face. I will especially help those whose end is near. I will be the goddess of awareness and of uncertainty."

She tilts the chalice and drinks. I see her swallow. She staggers as the drink runs through her, but my protecting wind keeps her from falling.

I am reeling myself. Kezi is safe. She comes into my arms —

But doesn't stay. Hannu dances to us and takes her hand. They dance into the aisles of tablets. I clasp Arduk's hand. We dance too, with Ursag joining in, then Puru, not holding anyone's hand, but following us in time with the rhythm of our feet, singing, "Fate . . . may . . . be . . . thwarted. Happy outcome. Glad fate. Fortunate Akka."

64
KEZI

Our dancing feet are loudest, but beyond them I hear voices, which I take to be the voices of the other gods. I even hear their breathing. I hear the winged steeds munching hay in the stable. Farther off are more voices. "Please . . ." ". . . rain . . ." ". . . old . . ." "Forgive . . ." They are prayers of Akkan mortals! So many I can't sort them out.

I see vast distances, too! It's hard to dance and *see.* A woman alone in a hut. A flock of sheep. Ursag's temple in Neme. I cling to Hannu's hand. I'm half blind with seeing and half deaf with hearing.

My nose is flooded. Familiar odors and odors I don't know. Most of all, the stinging scent of pine trees.

Hannu stops dancing and hugs me. "My daughter!"

When she lets me go, Olus tells everyone we must leave.

I do not ride Kastu. A winged horse would frighten the people of Hyte. On Olus's wind I teach myself to direct my eyes and ears.

Night is falling. Olus brings us to earth in a glade surrounded by evergreens. Twigs crack. Leaves rustle. Daytime animals are settling down.

We settle too, Olus a few inches away from me. I stare at the stars, which seem no closer than they ever did.

"How do you sleep through all the sounds?" I hear every night creature. I haven't stopped hearing Akkan voices, and now I hear snores and people rolling over.

"I'm accustomed to them; but when I was little, I imagined they were in my winds, and they put me to sleep."

After a few minutes of not falling asleep, I say, "I'm still afraid of the priest's knife. It will hurt, won't it, even though I'll live?"

"Yes. But the wound will heal quickly."

I wonder if Pado and Mati will be able to bear bringing me to the temple. Maybe they will decide to let me live.

They mustn't! If I'm not sacrificed, Pado's oath will become empty. Braving Wadir, becoming immortal, even saving Aunt Fedo will have been for nothing.

Olus says, "Kezi . . . we can't live in Hyte."

"No?" I think. "No. We can't." The priests and priestesses mustn't see me alive after my sacrifice. My family mustn't know, or they'll be terrified. So tomorrow will be my last time in Hyte with my family.

"You can knot rugs on Enshi Rock."

But my loom won't be next to Mati's. Aunt Fedo won't be sitting with us, describing what her owl eyes have seen. Pado won't be nearby in his counting room.

I'm being ungrateful. I say, "We'll be happy."

"We will." He adds, "But you'll miss them."

"Yes." I always will.

I listen to the notes and rhythms in the night. I picture a line of all the animals and people in Akka, dancing. In the middle of the imaginary line, stepping and gliding, are Mati and Pado and Aunt Fedo. I join them and slide into a dream.

When I wake up, it is my last day — would have been my last day. I awaken with an idea. I'm not a goddess of Hyte, but I can do something for the people of my city. The city that used to be mine.

As soon as we cross over the falls of Zago, I can see and hear as far as Hyte. I find my street. In the alley behind my pado's house, while beating rugs, Nia is praying that my sacrifice will be glorious. In his counting room Pado lies prostrate, praying for a sign that I may be spared. In our courtyard Mati and Aunt Fedo simply weep. None seem to doubt that I will return. Thank you for your faith in me.

Olus sets us down outside the city gates. No fire in the market today. No music. No pretend wool merchant to cause a miracle. We walk to my street. I am home.

65
OLUS

Kezi leans her forehead against the painted wood of her pado's door, then presses her whole body against it. Her hand finds mine as she pushes open the door. "Pado? Mati? Aunt Fedo?"

Merem is first into the reception room, then Senat, and last Aunt Fedo, who is the only one to see me. They engulf Kezi. The mass of them rocks back and forth. Senat's bass voice rumbles "Kezi" over and over. The reception room is small. I back into a corner next to the altar. In the faces of Kezi's parents and her aunt I see the lines of grief.

Finally they separate.

Senat says, "We searched everywhere for you."

Merem touches Kezi's hair. Then "Your tunic . . ." She bends down to examine the hem. "Gold —"

"You brought a guest," Aunt Fedo says.

Senat sees me. "Olus? Olus, the goatherd? Is that you?"

I nod. Merem and Aunt Fedo bow their heads politely to me. I raise my fist to my forehead.

"He knows," Kezi says. "Everything."

I feel my face redden.

Senat flushes too. "You know my shame."

"Kezi," Merem says, "why did you leave us?"

It's Kezi's turn to blush. "We were so sad. I had only a month. I didn't want to be sad every minute of my last month."

Merem nods. "Are you hungry?" She laughs, the same pained, ironic laugh as when she was sick. "You might as well eat." She addresses me. "Olus, have you broken your fast? We are hospitable to guests" — she laughs again — "no matter what."

Without waiting for an answer, she leads the way into the courtyard and from there to the eating room at the back of the house. Three chairs are pulled up to a square table from which the remains of breakfast have not yet been removed. Two servants bustle in from the kitchen. One clears the table. The other opens the doors to the alley behind the house. In wafts my mischievous breeze, stinking of refuse.

"Bring food for our guest and Kezi," Merem says.

"Bring chairs," Aunt Fedo adds. "Sit, Olus."

I look to Kezi to see if I should sit when there aren't enough chairs for all, but her eyes are on her family.

"Sit, Olus," Senat says.

"Thank you for your kindness." I sit and wish someone else would sit too, but they all stand. How can everything be so ordinary: the hospitality, the awkwardness of strangers?

A servant brings in a large barley cake, goat cheese, dates. Another servant carries in chairs. Everyone sits at last, Merem and Aunt Fedo on either side of Kezi. Senat rises immediately. He tells the servants to leave and gives each a task in a distant room of the house. Then he goes to the kitchen and sends the cook and his helper to the market. When he returns, Merem fills a plate for Kezi and me.

"Olus," Senat says, seating himself, "how do you come to be here with my daughter?"

We should have thought this out and decided what to say. "I was at your brother's wedding. I met Kezi there."

"I want to hear everything," Aunt Fedo says. "Olus and Kezi, speak slowly. There's

259

no hurry."

"Yes, slowly," Mati says. "The priest can wait."

Senat glances obliquely at the altar flame and says nothing.

Mati moves her chair close to Kezi's and touches her cheek. "Nothing is as soft."

Kezi catches her mati's hand and holds it.

Senat says, "My eyes have ached from not seeing my Kezi."

"Aren't you going to eat, Pado? Mati? Aunt Fedo?" Kezi leans over the table and puts food on a plate for each of them. "A large slice of barley cake for Aunt Fedo."

Aunt Fedo says, "Your voice is different, Kezi. My rabbit ears hear — I'm not certain — an echo. Why is that?"

Kezi shrugs. It's the goddess in her voice.

No one eats.

"Speak, daughter," Senat says.

She nods. "Aunt Fedo introduced me to Elon. Remember?"

"I remember. He was so eager to meet you!"

I hear people in the street outside the red door. A dozen priests are coming.

"He persuaded me to walk —"

"Go on," Merem says.

"Listen . . . do you hear?"

The street door opens. The priests hurry

across the courtyard. A priest knocks over a potted fern. Everyone hears the crash.

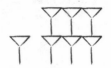

66
KEZI

The priests are clad in yellow tunics. The first one to enter wears a silver necklace. A high priest. He has a squared-off black beard and wears a curled wig as the asupu did.

Pado stands. Mati moves her chair closer to mine and doesn't let my hand go.

"Senat . . ." the high priest says. He knows Pado. "We've come for your daughter."

Mati's grip tightens. "Take me! I shouldn't have —"

Aunt Fedo pounds her cane. "Take me. I would —"

Pado commands, "Hush!" To the high priest he says, "Wait, Lesu," and goes to the eating-room altar. "Admat, send a sign. We beg your mercy." He prostrates himself. "Send a sign that my daughter need not die. Send a sign that no one need die. As you wish, so it will be."

I feel a breeze. The flame flares. Dies down. Flares again. Dies down.

I look at Olus and know. He is causing the flares.

The flame brightens a third time. Maybe I can escape this Lesu's knife and we can stay in Hyte. I look at Mati, whose face is awed.

Pado rises. "Admat —"

Lesu intones, "Admat has revealed himself. Admat accepts the sacrifice."

Oh no!

Does Lesu have a way of understanding Admat? Or does he himself want me sacrificed?

Pado says, "Lesu —"

He interrupts. "As he wishes, so it shall be. Senat, it is Admat's wish. You know, or you wouldn't have told me to come today."

The breath flies out of me.

"You called him?" Mati yells.

"I knew I wouldn't be able to send for the priest after you came," Pado tells me. "I had to do it before." He's weeping. "Kezi, 'Admat's wrath is worse than death.' "

I nod. He is quoting the holy text. The words that follow are *Admat's love is better than life.* Pado loves me. He just believes what I used to believe. I remind myself that we came home for me to be sacrificed.

Olus's face is furious. I fear he will do

something terrible with his winds. I say, "I accept my sacrifice," and catch his eye.

His expression softens. "So it will be."

Lesu says, "Admat is pleased."

How does he know?

I strengthen the echo Aunt Fedo heard in my voice. Louder than I used to be able to speak, I pronounce, "So it will be, but remember these words: Admat hates human sacrifice." This was my idea when I awoke this morning. "My sacrifice will be the last. Admat loves the people of Hyte. He is not a punishing god. He never brings anyone suffering."

"I will not argue theology with the sacrifice," Lesu says. "Come."

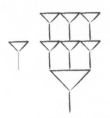

67

OLUS

Lesu leads us out of Senat's house as if he owned it. In the street Kezi walks with her mati and aunt. Aunt Fedo leans heavily on her cane, her limp worse than usual. Merem's arm is around her daughter. Senat and I follow them. Lesu and the other priests form a loose circle around us.

People stare. A stray dog trots at Lesu's side.

I have to restrain my winds, which want what I want: to cast the priests and even Senat into the desert, to blind them with sand, to deafen them, to make them feel the wrath of this god.

The temple rises ahead, blocky and graceless. We enter through groaning bronze doors into a vestibule, and from there into a windowless room hardly big enough to contain us. I wouldn't have been able to stay here for even a moment before my trial.

Lesu asks Senat, "What is the sacrifice's name?"

"My name" — she waits until he meets her eyes — "is Kezi. I am a weaver. I love to dance." She raises her arms. There's no space to dance, but she kicks out her left foot, then her right.

Merem sobs.

Senat says, "When I swore the oath, I thought —"

"Kezi will come with me now. It won't —"

"I'm her mati," Merem says. "Her mati should be by her —"

"Quiet!"

"I gave her life. I —"

"Quiet. Senat may stay during the ceremony . . ." His voice becomes less formal. Briefly, he stops being his office. "Although I think you'd best not."

I can come too. If I use my winds, no one can prevent me. But I do nothing. I'll see and hear everything. She knows I'll be with her from here.

"Will it . . ." Aunt Fedo raps her cane on the floor. "Will it . . ." She raps the cane again to make her words come out. "Will it . . . hurt?"

266

"Admat will dull the pain," Lesu says.

Perhaps when this is over, I will kill him and Admat will dull his pain.

Kezi rushes into her aunt's arms. "Don't worry, Aunt Fedo. Good-bye." She embraces her mati. "Good-bye, Mati." She holds her hands out to me. "I must tell you good-bye." So softly that no one but a god can hear, she whispers, "Can Admat kill a god?"

I shout, "No!"

Kezi nods. To Lesu she says, "The sacrifice is ready."

Yet an all-powerful god probably can kill an Akkan god anywhere, any time. If Admat exists and if he is wrathful, there is no escape.

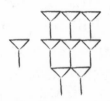

68
KEZI

I can tell Olus isn't certain. In spite of everything, I may die.

Admat, don't kill me! Don't be wrathful. Don't exist!

Lesu takes Pado and me to the liver-shaped central prayer room. We enter through the small door behind the altar. Across the room are the double doors that are opened only twice a year.

A screen stands between the altar and the wall. Lesu tells me to go behind it.

A priestess waits there. She raises my tunic and examines me without saying a word. She seems unaware of the blush that covers every inch of my skin.

Let her find something wrong. Make me unfit to be a sacrifice. I point out a birth-mark on my ankle. She runs her thumb across it, presses it, and then continues her inspection. Her hands turn me, lift my right leg, lift my left, while I try to think of another flaw. I show her the scar of an old cut on my forearm. This she barely looks at. She isn't gentle or rough. I am simply a task.

Finally she lowers the tunic. We come out from behind the screen. She tells Lesu that I'm "acceptable."

Two priests lift me onto the altar. I stiffen. I didn't realize, but until now I thought something would keep this moment from coming. My ears buzz. My temples pound. I ball my fists — tight, tight, tight — to keep from screaming.

The priestess places oil lamps around me. I turn my head so I can see Pado.

He gazes back. I don't look away and neither does he. Someone lights the lamps. I feel their heat. I smell incense. Lesu chants:

"Admat, the one, the all,
Accept this offering and
Send your blessings to Hyte.
Accept this oath repayment and
Send your blessings to Hyte.
Accept this girl and
Send your blessings to Hyte."

Pado doesn't blink. He is with me, as I

know Olus and Mati and Aunt Fedo are. Olus sees me. He'll see the knife come down. I won't. I'll see only my pado's eyes.

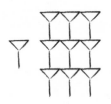

69
OLUS

The knife descends. Kezi's blood spurts. My own blood throbs in my ears. She moans. I shout. Her aunt and mati clutch each other.

Kezi continues to stare fixedly at her pado. Has she died? Has Admat —

No! She still breathes — shallowly. Her chest rises and falls, imperceptibly except to me. She must be in such pain, but after the one moan she is silent.

The priestess closes her eyes. Lesu takes Senat's hand and tugs him from the room. The high priest tells Senat, "Her sacred body will be washed. We will pray over it today and . . ."

They won't!

My gusty wind blows open the double doors to the room that holds her. My cradling wind and my gentle wind pick her up and waft her through several small rooms — but not the one we're crowded in — between the open bronze doors, into the sky, and away to Enshi Rock.

I say farewell to Merem and Aunt Fedo, although I doubt they hear me. From the temple I walk to the gates of Hyte. All the while, I listen to Kezi's weak breaths.

After
Kezi

Years have passed.

When I reached Enshi Rock after my sacrifice, the goddess of medicine nursed me back to health. The god of forgetfulness offered to mist my sacrifice, but I told him not to. Since my days in Wadir I've wanted to remember everything.

As soon as I was well enough, Olus and I married. The ceremony was performed at Olus's temple in Akka, so our worshipers could attend. I even coaxed a few mortal women to dance with me. Kudiya was the only mortal man brave enough to dance with Olus and the gods. In the wedding pantomime Puru, of all gods, took the part of Gossip and enthusiastically clapped together the donkey's jawbones. Nin, the storm goddess, was Storm, naturally, and the war god was War. Hannu and Arduk pretended to be the arguing children.

Our most unusual wedding guests were

Olus's goats. He says they deserve his gratitude for bringing us together. Arduk provided delicious grass and herbs for them.

Everything would have been perfect if Mati and Pado and Aunt Fedo could have taken part.

I often watch and listen to them from the falls of Zago. They suffered, Pado most of all. Mati blamed herself for making so much of her illness. Aunt Fedo blamed herself for forcing her way into our house. Pado blamed himself for everything.

At first their sole comfort was in the disappearance of my body from the temple. They hoped that the miracle was a sign of Admat's forgiveness and of my forgiveness.

I asked the goddess of sleep to send them dreams. She sent dreams of me laughing, dancing, knotting rugs. After my children were born, the goddess sent dreams of them, too. The dreams consoled my parents and Aunt Fedo.

The priests and priestesses of Hyte also call my disappearance a miracle. Some people believe that Admat took me to Wadir to become his wife, and they worship me!

Everyone looks on my words about human sacrifice as truth. Even the holy text has been changed.

I ride Kastu to my temple in Akka every

week. The temple has a red door, just as the houses in Hyte do. The walls are hung with rugs. Some rugs I made and some were offerings of other weavers. Hannu sent pots, and Arduk filled them with flowers that never die. Olus's winds blow in spicy and sweet scents. Musicians and dancers practice their arts in my courtyard. They are welcome, as long as they let the unskilled join in.

My temple has a quiet room for conversation. People talk more easily to me than to the other gods, because they know I used to be mortal. They tell me their questions, and I tell them mine, and we wonder together.

Olus and I raised three daughters and three sons. All were born mortal. Ursag says it's because I was born mortal. Two sons and one daughter chose to drink therka and were able to swallow it. The others chose not to drink and remained mortal. I am glad for those who will live eternally and for those whose lives will be fleeting. Death in old age is often welcome. My mortal children will help populate the earth.

For one month in twelve I seek Admat. It is a sacred quest, but thus far I haven't found him. The god of everywhere and everything remains hidden. Olus always accompanies me on my searches. Puru sometimes gives us puzzling advice.

I know that fate may be thwarted. We strive for happy outcomes.

ABOUT THE AUTHOR

Gail Carson Levine grew up in New York City and has been writing all her life. Her first book for children, *Ella Enchanted,* was a Newbery Honor Book. Levine's other books include *Fairest,* a *New York Times* bestseller, *Publishers Weekly* Best Book of the Year, and *School Library Journal* Best Book of the Year; *Dave at Night,* an ALA Notable Book and Best Book for Young Adults; *The Wish; The Two Princesses of Bamarre;* and the six Princess Tales books. She is also the author of the non-fiction book *Writing Magic: Creating Stories That Fly* and the picture book *Betsy Who Cried Wolf,* illustrated by Scott Nash. Gail, her husband, David, and their Airedale, Baxter, live in a 217-year-old farmhouse in the Hudson Valley of New York State. You can visit her online at www.gailcarsonlevinebooks.com.